Ushi rolled on her tummy and took off her shades to get a better look up the beach. It was filling up and she couldn't see Stella anywhere. She could see loads of talent, though. Just as she'd predicted. Oooooh yes, that guy presently walking up the beach in their direction . . . With his cropped blond hair and tanned, everso taut body, he really was something else. Problem was he was holding the hand of a rather lovely, tall, dark girl dressed in a rather lovely, pale-yellow bikini. Ushi sat up suddenly. She recognised that bikini! She ought to. It was hers. She'd lent it to Stella a few hours earlier. Well, well, well, lucky old Stell! With a lad like that in tow, no wonder she'd forgotten all about their ice creams . . .

J·17

Girls On Tour

Just Seventeen

Triple Trouble

The Red-Hot Love Hunt

Too Hot To Handle

Double-Cross Dilemma

Love Games

Girls On Tour

J-17

Girls On Tour

by Alison James

RED FOX

For Frank, Charlie and Olivia

A Red Fox Book

Published by Random House Children's Books
20 Vauxhall Bridge Road, London SW1V 2SA

A division of Random House UK Ltd
London Melbourne Sydney Auckland
Johannesburg and agencies throughout the world

Copyright © Alison James 1997

1 3 5 7 9 10 8 6 4 2

First published in Great Britain by Red Fox 1997

Typeset in by Sabon by
Palimpsest Book Production Limited,
Polmont, Stirlingshire
Printed and bound in Great Britain by
Cox & Wyman Ltd, Reading, Berkshire

Papers used by Random House UK Limited are natural,
recyclable products made from wood grown in sustainable
forests. The manufacturing processes conform to the
environmental regulations of the country of origin.

RANDOM HOUSE UK Limited Reg. No. 954009

ISBN 0 09 925152 3

♥

Bon Voyage!

Grey skies, an even greyer sea, gale-force winds and a ferry that seemed about as stable and secure as a toy boat in a jacuzzi. It was not, Jodie reflected, clinging to the deck rail and chucking her guts up for what had to be the fifth time in almost as many minutes, supposed to be like this. Not when yesterday she'd forked out a load of dosh on a new 'do' which didn't exactly lend itself to the windswept look. Not when her gorgeous new strappy dress wasn't wind and salt-water resistant. And especially not when she'd done as her mum had suggested and had dosed up on seasick pills which tasted bad enough on the way down, let alone on the way back up again!

A real waste of money they'd been. And the same could be said for the 'all day full English breakfast' she'd scoffed less than half-an-hour ago. A regurgitated £6.99's worth was now adrift somewhere in the English Channel. Mmmmm! Yummy! Lucky fish! That's if there were any fish actually alive in water this murky.

The only consolation was that she wasn't the only one who was suffering. Stella and Ushi, the other two members of their 'girl gang' trio – the 'unholy trinity' as they called themselves – Jodie's absolute best mates with whom she'd come away, had just ralphed up their insides too.

'Oh my God, I think I'm a goner,' moaned Ushi, sinking down onto the deck, her thick hair falling forward across her heart-shaped face while her cut-offs and tiny T-shirt were, like Jodie's dress, completely soaked through. 'Why, oh why didn't we take the flamin' chunnel?'

''Cos it cost too much,' groaned Stella, shakily wiping her mouth with a tissue. 'I'd have gladly paid it if I'd known it was going to be as rough as this, though.'

'No point crying over spilt milk,' Jodie sighed.

'Aw, don't,' muttered Ushi. 'Yeuchh! The thought of off-milk! You'll set me off again!' She took a long, grateful slurp of *eau minerale*. 'Call me a travel dyslexic but I never imagined the crossing between Dover and Boulogne would be this dodgy. It's summer, for crying out loud! I thought we'd be sunning our selves and sipping cocktails, not freezing our butts off and losing our lunch!'

'The mysteries of the sea,' intoned Stella mysteriously. 'Who can predict her tempestuous moods?'

'Eh?' muttered Jodie.

Stella grinned. 'I once wrote a poem about the sea – got an "A" for it, too.'

'Yeah, well . . .' went on Ushi. 'I'm just grateful there'll be no more boats after this one. And no more moody seas, either. We'll be InterRailing, won't we? And who's ever heard of anyone getting train sick?'

'A whole month!' sighed Stella dreamily. 'Can you really believe it yet? I can't. After all those months of planning and talking about it, we're finally doing it. Training our way across Europe for four fantastic weeks. It's going to be a-bloody-mazing. No mardy parents sticking their beaks in where they're not wanted, no college, no boring nights in in front of the telly. But fun, fun, fun! Sightseeing, shopping, scoffing down the local delicacies and . . .'

'Loads-a-lads,' Jodie finished for her. 'Mmmm! Yes please! Foreign fare – and I'm not talking frogs' legs or spag bog, either. It'll be like being let loose in a kind of dream deli. Lean, luscious blonds from Scandanavia, horny *Herren* from Germany, fabulous French men, gorgeous Greeks . . . Ooh yeah, all that hot-blooded totty from the Med. And that's not including the scores of sun-kissed, snog-hungry Brits we're bound to run into, too.'

Easing herself upright, Ushi suddenly looked out to sea. She smiled. 'Forget boys for a mo', me old ship maties! Be it my imagination or has this here vessel stopped rocking n'rolling a tad?'

Jodie hauled herself up and followed Ushi's gaze. Yep, she was right. The wind had dropped and the waves were now lapping gently against the ship's hull rather than threatening to come aboard.

'Affirmative, I'm glad to say.'

'Well hallejuiah for that,' whooped Stella, getting up and tentatively testing out her sea legs. 'I thought we'd be stuck up here for the duration. So little time and so much to see! The games room looked pretty happening and we haven't even touched the duty free yet. My pulse points are just itching to be dabbed with criminally-expensive perfume. Then . . .' she grinned wickedly at the other two, her dark eyes flashing like black diamonds, 'there's the bar . . .'

'Oh yeah?' teased Jodie. 'And what's so special about the bar? As if I didn't know!'

'Posh totty!' Ushi answered excitedly. She held out a hand and Jodie pulled her up. 'That's if they're still there. Three gorge guys. All floppy hair, fresh faces and clipped vowels. Not our usual types, perhaps, but we're on holiday and you know what they say, a change is as good as a rest. Mmmmm . . .' she licked her lips thoughtfully, 'I've never snogged a posh lad before. Wonder what it's like.'

'Absolutely spiffing,' chortled Jodie. 'I bet you can tell a pedigree tongue a mile orf!'

Stella had already started running down the deck. 'What are you waiting for, darlings?' she yelled back over her shoulder. 'If I've got anything to do with it, we're all about to find out!'

'InterRailing round Europe, huh?' the poshest of the three posh-lads smarmed. 'For a month? *Quelle coïncidence, lay-deez. Nous aussi.* My friends and I would be more than happy to accompany *medmoiselles* some of the way.'

Jodie looked at Ushi and Stella, not at all surprised to see that they looked as hacked-off as she felt. What an idiot! Correction. What a trio of idiots! They'd been sitting in the bar with this threesome for the best part of half-an-hour yet Smarm-Features only just seemed to have picked up on the fact that they were InterRailing too. Talk about tedious! He and his mates had been too busy fiddling around with their mobile phones and talking about themselves to absorb information about anyone else. Too busy sounding off about such-and-such a ball and all these 'Taras' and 'Tamaras' who, apparently, found them absolutely irresistible.

'Anyone else noticed that a pack of pigs have just taken flight?' Ushi had quipped at that point.

Jodie and Stella had laughed but not a flicker of mirth had passed across the chaps' mugs. God, they were so arrogant, so up themselves, Jodie considered – not for the first time – that if the interior wasn't up to much, then the exterior – however gorge it might be – didn't count for a whole lot, either. What's more, she was pretty damned sure that the toff-type accents weren't all they seemed. Nobody talked *that* posh – never mind plums, these guys had bricks in their mouths. Not only that, they were way, way, out of date.

'Yuppies,' she wanted to say, 'went out with shoulder pads.'

'Yah,' Smarm-Features brayed on. 'We could act as your knights in shining armour. Real three musketeer stuff. *Mon Dieu*, it is not always safe out there for pretty lay-deez like yourselves.'

'You're right there,' Stella muttered. 'Not with the likes of you on the loose.'

Jodie bit into her hand to stop herself from laughing out loud. So what if they were prime prats? All the better to have some laughs with – or rather at.

'Sorry?' one of them asked Stella. 'I didn't quite catch that.'

'Juice!' Ushi interrupted suddenly. 'She'd like some orange juice. Here Stell, have one of these.'

Trying unsuccessfully not to giggle, Ushi handed Stella one of the cartons that was on the table.

'Actually, they're mine,' piped up one of the posh lads. 'I bought them earlier. You're welcome to buy one off me though, if you like.'

Jodie shook her head in disbelief. Was he for real? Apparently so – God, what a tightarse!'

'Forget it!' muttered Ushi.

'Oh my,' Stella looked at her watch and yawned. 'Doesn't time fly when you're having fun. Not!'

'Know something?' Ushi suddenly announced. 'I feel a bit sick again. In fact,' she got up from the table and lurched towards Smarm-Features, 'I think I'm going to . . .' She made a retching noise in her throat.

'Oh for God's sake!'

Smarm-Features moved his chair away from her. Jodie started to laugh out loud. Ushi could be a real a law unto herself at times.

Staggering around the bar as if the storm really had blown up again, Ushi stumbled out through the door. Jodie and Stella looked at each other then got up to follow her.

'See you, er, Jodie,' Smarm-Features called after them. Stella nudged her. Jodie pulled a face.

'Not if I see you first,' she muttered under her breath and, catching Stella's arm, the two of them walked swiftly out of the bar without a backward glance.

They expected to find Ushi waiting for them but she was nowhere to be seen.

'She'll have gone to the duty free shop,' said Stella. 'She'll be spraying herself like there's no tomorrow.'

But she wasn't. Stella and Jodie spent some time sniffing and sampling the scores of bottles on offer before deciding they'd better look for Ushi. They scoured the loos – on all four decks – the games room, the numerous lounges, restaurants and cafés, the duty free shop (again!) and completely circumnavigated the exterior deck area. But no Ushi. It was weird. In fact two things were weird – the way Ushi had just disappeared and the spooky way the wind had started to blow strongly again. It was almost as if Ushi had prophesied it. Where the hell was she? In the end, they were forced to go back to the bar to ask Smarm-Features and his divvy mates if they'd seen her.

''Fraid not, Jodie m'dear,' he slimed. 'Not that she'd be sitting with us, anyway. Methinks we come from very different places.'

Methinks?!!! Just what was that tosser on?

'Methinks he fancies you, "Jodie m'dear",' chuckled Stella once they were out of his hearing.

'I know – worst luck,' Jodie grimaced.

'You know, it's a shame he wasn't out on deck when it was dead rough,' Stella went on. 'He could have gone for a dip.'

Jodie's face filled with worry. 'Don't say that, Stell. What if that's what's happened to Ushi? She could have gone out on deck when she left the bar. Who knows? Maybe she really did start to feel sick again. Well, the wind *had* just started to blow again, hadn't it? Say she went up to the top deck. Say a sudden gust knocked her off balance. There'd only be one place for her to fall, wouldn't there? And she's not a strong swimmer, is she?'

'Don't be ridiculous, Jodes,' said Stella. 'We'll have one more look around then we'll go see the captain or whoever. Get a message put out over the tannoy.' She put an arm around Jodie. 'Don't get your knickers in a twist – she'll turn up.'

But having circumnavigated the ship a second time and still no Ushi, Jodie had gone into major fret mode and Stella, too, was starting to get a bit niggled.

'What are we going to tell her mum?' Jodie whined. 'We can't just ring up and say, "Sorry, your daughter's fallen off the ferry".'

'Who's fallen off the ferry?' It was Ushi. She grinned. 'Anyone I know?'

Jodie grabbed Ushi and flung her arms around her. 'You're safe! Thank God! We thought you'd fallen overboard.'

'Eh?' Ushi looked bemused.

'We!' Stella exclaimed. 'You, y'mean. Where've you been anyway, Ushi?' Stella scolded. 'We've been looking everywhere for you.'

'Ditto,' replied Ushi. 'When I left the bar, I went to the loo. Then I peeped through the bar door to see if you were still with those creeps. You weren't so I went looking for you. When I couldn't find you, I figured we'd meet up eventually so I decided to chill out and write some postcards until we did.'

She sat down in the nearest chair and threw a couple of cards onto the table.

'Already?' Stella asked. 'We only left home this morning. Who've you been writing to?' She picked one up.

'*Snake Hips*,' she read aloud. '"*It's only been a few hours but I miss you like mad*" . . . Blimey, Ush, who the hell's "Snake Hips" when he's at home?'

'Davy,' beamed Ushi. 'You know, that lad I copped off with the other night. He's soooo gorgeous. Call it forward planning but I want to keep him sweet for when we get home. No post-holiday blues for me, girls!'

'So does that mean no holiday romances, either?' enquired Stella. 'If you're keeping yourself sweet for him?'

'Does it hell,' grinned Ushi. 'But what darling Davy doesn't know won't hurt him, will it?'

Jodie shook her head. 'You're what my gran would call a caution, Ushi,' she tutted and sat down at the table with the others. 'It'll all end in tears. Still, never mind about that now. We're all together again so what better time than to work out exactly where we're heading. I mean, we've discussed it often enough but we still have to work out a definite route. Or should that be the definitive route? Well, whatever, either way, we haven't done it yet . . .'

'OK, so where's it going to be?' Ushi reached into her bag, pulled out a map of Europe and spread it across the table. 'Now where did we kind-of agree on last time? Oh yeah . . .' Her fingers started to walk across the map in a westerly direction. 'Once we've arrived in Boulogne, we go to Lille so we can catch a train to Brittany – so that means we're in north west France . . . Then, we move diagonally across country to the Riviera and down into Italy. Yes please!' She shivered deliciously. 'All those divine Latino boys called Carlo and Giovanni. Even their names are sexy. Anyway, where to when we've been there? Is there indeed anywhere worth going after *la bella Italia*.'

'Sure is,' piped up Jodie. 'What about Greece?'

'Mmmm, could be tricky,' mused Ushi. 'I fancy it but it'll mean taking another ferry from – where it is now? – oh yeah, Brindisi. Do we mind about that? What d'you think, Stella? Stell, what's up? You've gone really quiet.'

Jodie looked at Stella. Her usually olivey complexion had turned pink and she looked kind of embarrassed.

'France is OK,' she muttered. 'I mean, it's fine. It's just that . . . when we hit the Riviera we might have to turn right rather than left. In fact . . .' Pink turned to deepest crimson. 'We'd probably do best to skip the Riviera altogether.'

'Why?' asked Jodie and Ushi at the same time.

'Because . . .' Stella shifted uncomfortably in her seat. 'I mean . . . Look, who does this remind you of?' She stood up, slightly stooped her shoulders and pulled on an imaginary cigar. '*You think I mad? I let you go round Europe for a month with just those friends of yours? Nice girls they are but they just girls. Like you. You think you a woman, Stella but you not. You just seventeen. You just a baby. OK, I let you go but on one condition. You go stay with your aunt Maria in España. For one week. I insist. Then I know you all right.*'

Jodie and Ushi stared at her blankly.

'It's my dad,' Stella sighed exasperated. 'I suppose I should have told you before,' Stella started fiddling nervously with her hair. 'But I was just too embarrassed. And a bit ashamed.'

'About what?' Jodie asked, still looking some-what confused. 'Come on, Stell, you can tell us. We're your friends, remember.'

'Your best friends,' added Ushi. '"One For All" and all that.'

Stella smiled gratefully. 'It's just that my parents said they'd only let me come away with you on one condition. Basically, we've got to go to Spain for a bit and stay with my auntie. So she can see for her-self that I'm all right and report back to my olds.'

'Well that's OK,' Ushi laughed. 'Blimey, I thought you were going to say something really awful. Going to Spain probably knocks Greece on the head but Spain or Italy? It doesn't really matter, does it? They're both mighty fine places. Yeah! Spain! *Olé!* Thinking about it, I quite like the names Javier and Julio, too. We'll find a happening beach and have ourselves a ball.'

'Er, that's unlikely at Aunt Maria's,' Stella went on. 'It's not exactly the grooviest place on earth. I've been before but not for a good few years now. It's actually inland, high up in the Pyrenees. What I'm trying to say is that it's miles from anywhere. In the middle of nowhere, in fact.'

'High up in the Pyrenees . . .' repeated Jodie dreamily. 'It sounds really romantic.'

'Yeah, it does,' agreed Ushi. 'But is there anyone to be romantic with, I wonder.'

'Dunno,' Stella shrugged. She started to giggle. 'There's Miguel, my cousin, but he's a real jerk. He's a few years older than me but I remember him as being a weedy, little cry baby. He's . . .'

She was suddenly interrupted by an annoucement coming over the tannoy.

'*We will shortly be arriving in Boulogne. Will passengers ensure that they have all their belongings . . .*'

They didn't stop to hear any more but rushed out onto the nearest deck. It was just getting dark and the lights of Boulogne flickered like stars across the water. Instinctively, Jodie grabbed Ushi and Stella and hugged them.

'This is it!' she squealed, her heart pounding with excitement.

They'd arrived! And this was only the beginning. France, Europe, the Continent beckoned. For a whole month, it would belong to them.

Just as was written in Jodie's travel guide, Boulogne train station was literally next to the port. She didn't know why she should be surprised but she was. Excitement, she supposed. And she sure was excited. France – her first time on foreign soil

– and she could hardly contain herself. Running backwards and forwards, pointing at all the signs, straining to hear people speak. In French! Suddenly she was glad that she'd always been pretty good at it. She wanted to see everything, experience everything. A mere hour-and-a-half away from old Blighty yet it was so, so different. It even smelled different – of French cigarettes and strong coffee.

She knew Ushi and Stella were watching her indulgently – she was the novice traveller while they'd both been abroad before – but this was a first for them, too. The first time any of them had been abroad without parents – or parenty-type figures – and it was hugely, fabulously liberating.

'We can do anything we want,' sang Ushi, dancing onto the station platform. 'No "what-time-d'you-call-this", no "you-treat-this-place-like-a-hotel", no "get-off-the-bloody-phone". God it's fantastic!'

Jodie gasped as Stella suddenly pushed her and Ushi behind an advertisement hoarding.

'What the hell's going on?' spluttered Ushi.

'I'm saving you from a fate worse than death, that's what,' hissed Stella. 'Smarm-Features and his slimey mates have just passed by. They're railing-it too, remember. Get stuck on a train with 'em now and the odds are we'll be stuck for the duration. And that I do not want.'

'*Absolument*,' agreed Jodie and Ushi nodded solemnly.

They were momentarily tempted to miss their train and get down to some serious bar-crawling in Boulogne but they figured there'd be plenty of time for that over the next four weeks.

'Miss this train,' Jodie said, squinting at the timetable, 'and we miss our connection from Lille to Brittany – and sun, sand and sea – in the morning.'

Sitting aboard the swank SNCF train as it travelled through the, now dark, French countryside, Jodie reckoned that she'd never been so thrilled about sitting on a train before. She kept touching the blue leather seats and peering out the window – even though she could see nothing but her own reflection. And it was so fast, it made trains at home seem like something out of the dark ages!

'The campsite's about 10 km outside Lille,' said Ushi, reading up in her *Camping Guide to France*. 'In a place called Malée. Even better, apparently it's only a few minutes walk from the station. We'll save on taxi fares and have some decent nosh instead. Don't know about you guys but suddenly I'm starving!'

On leaving Malée station, the three of them followed the directions in Ushi's book. True to its word – thank God, as they were hauling rucksacks on their backs – it was only minutes away. But there was a problem. It had started to rain. Tiny little spits at first which rapidly metamorphosed into puddle-size sploshes.

'Hurrah!' muttered Stella as they stumbled into the campsite reception just as an almighty crash of thunder sounded.

'*Ah bonsoir*,' the woman behind the desk started to say then, suddenly, everything went dark. The three of them screamed.

'*Ah c'est une coupure de courant* – a, how-you-say, power cut,' the woman went on as if it was the most usual thing in the world. Maybe, Jodie thought, it was here. The woman lit one candle and gave another to Ushi.

'Er thanks,' muttered Ushi. 'A candle, eh? For use in the rain. Mmmm – very useful.'

The woman walked over and opened the door.

'Er, p'raps we should stay put till the rain slackens off a bit,' suggested Stella.

'Nice idea,' muttered Ushi, 'but I don't exactly

think that's what she has in mind. Look at her, beckoning us over. She's desperate for us to go. We've got no option, I'm afraid.'

Struggling with her rucksack, Jodie followed Stella and Ushi into the dark, wet night towards their appointed pitch. Detaching their sleeping bags and fiddling around with ground sheets, tent pegs and guide ropes by only the light of a torch during what felt like a mini-monsoon wasn't ideal. Some of Jodie's excitement had started to ebb away. She hadn't imagined this particular scenario when, tucked up in her bed at home, she'd fantasised about their very first night away. She'd imagined a perfectly put-up tent amidst a perfectly beautiful setting with a wonderful café that did a mean veg curry – just what she fancied. But when she mentioned food to Stella, she just laughed.

'You're joking, Jodes,' muttered Stella, attempting – unsuccessfully – to slip over the tent's top sheet. 'No power equals no scoff, I reckon. Don't you?'

'Oh don't say that,' moaned Ushi. 'My stomach's about to go on strike if it doesn't get any food.'

'Yeah, you're right,' said Stella. 'Hunger strike. There's no food, Ush. How can there be?'

'Well that's just great!' Ushi threw down a handful of pegs.

'It's not my fault,' Stella snapped back.

'I didn't say it was, did I?' hissed Ushi.

Jodie took a step back and her foot came into contact with something far squashier than grass – however wet. For a second, she couldn't make out exactly what it was but then came the horrible realisation that there was only one – or rather three – things it could be.

'Er, guys,' she said as the others continued to bicker. 'Guys . . .' This time a little louder.

Stella and Ushi looked at her.

'What?' they both snapped.

As gently as she could, Jodie broke it to them that their sleeping bags had been left out in the rain, uncovered, and were now, as indeed, were the three of them, completely drenched. As Jodie attempted to catch some zzzzzzs an hour or so later, shivering with cold, soaked through and starving hungry, she reflected that the feeling of intense excitement she'd been carrying around all day that had reached a crescendo on arriving in France, had disappeared completely. She and Ushi and Stella were barely talking to each other – each blaming the other for forgetting about the sleeping bags, the torrential rain, the lack of food – everything, in fact. No, she thought, it wasn't supposed to be like this at all. It was turning out to be a complete disaster.

♥

Life's A Beach

Hi Davy! ♡
Just had to write to you! Looked
at my watch and realised that
precisely six minutes, twelve
hours and two days ago we were
sitting under that weeping
willow having our farewell snog.
Awww! I don't half miss those
snogsome lips of yours! Stopped
in a disgusting campsite last night-
no food but loads of rain. Yeah, I
know - you're having a heatwave
back home! Don't think I'm a natural
under canvas - only under weeping
willows! Love and kisses xxx
♡ Ushi ♡

'Not *another* postcard!'

Ushi glanced up to see Stella grinning at her from
the other side of the train.

'Oh, you're talking to me now, are you?' muttered Ushi.

Stella grinned again. 'I've had a sleep and I feel better. Sorry for being so grumpy this morning but I'm never at my best before about half eleven, especially when I've hardly had any sleep the night before. And I reckon last night was the mother of all sleepless nights.'

'You're not wrong there,' said Ushi and put down her pen. 'Just let's promise ourselves one thing and then forget all about it. Tonight we stay in a hotel. I don't care how much it costs, I just need to get some kip.'

'*Absolument, ma chère*,' agreed Stella.

Ushi yawned and looked out the window. Having picked up their connection at Lille a few hours earlier, they were now en route to Brittany. The rain had stopped, the sun was shining and as they travelled further west, through Normandy into Brittany, the scenery became more and more lush and picturesque.

'This,' thought Ushi, the previous night suddenly becoming little more than a bad dream, 'is the life.'

'Coffee?' Ushi smiled up at Jodie who had just walked into the carriage, carrying a steaming tray.

'You bet!' Ushi murmured and took a cup. 'Oh Jodes, you've bought biccies, too! What a star!'

Jodie gave a mock curtsey and passed the tray to Stella. 'You know, maybe it wasn't such a bright idea to jump on the first train that was leaving Lille station in vaguely the right direction,' said Jodie. 'I asked the girl in the refreshment car where exactly we're going but she started babbling away so quickly, I couldn't keep up with her. I think she said something about a place called St Marion.'

Ushi started flicking through her guide book.

'We're going to Brittany, aren't we?' she said.

'Brittany's a big place,' said Stella. 'A bit like a county.'

'Oh anywhere'll do,' said Ushi airily. 'Just so long as there's a beautiful beach where we can chill out for a day or so, there aren't loads of pesky little kids running around and there's a decent hotel.'

'*Excusez-moi*, but I zink I may be able to 'elp you.'

Ushi looked up and found herself staring up into a pair of sexy brown eyes. The rest of their owner's face wasn't bad, either. A wide, full-lipped mouth, neat aquiline nose and a pair of cheek-bones you could balance a tray on – all topped off with a curly mane of shoulder-length dark hair. Then there was his body – that was amazing! Lean with long, long legs – gift-wrapped in a pair of faded denims and white T-shirt.

Ushi closed her eyes for an instant, thinking she must be dreaming. But when she opened them again, he was still there. Mr Completely Gorgeous – what a result! And, there was an added bonus too – the French accent may be undeniably corny but it was dead horny, too.

'I 'ope you don't mind me interrupting but I over 'ear you,' he said. 'You look for somewhere in Brittany with ze beautiful beach? I zink I can 'elp.'

Ushi glanced at Stella and Jodie. They grinned at her and Jodie gave her a sneaky 'thumbs-up'.

'I am François.' He held out a hand to her. '*Et vous?*'

Ushi told him her name and then introduced him to the others.

'Where's this place . . .' Ushi looked at the guide book again, 'er, St Marion?'

Sitting down to join them, François shook his head. St Marion, he informed them, was too touristy, too commercialised. He apparently knew of an unspoilt seaside village just inside the Brittany border which, apparently, was something of a hot secret.

'It is so very special, so very *naturel*,' he went on. 'You will not find it in any brochure. I go there – I meet some friends. We 'ang out. I camp, but there is a small 'otel there. Small, cheap . . .'

'Sounds great,' enthused Ushi. Fab beach and an even fabber boy-babe she fancied getting to know better. Paradise!

François shrugged. 'I get coffee now. You tell me when I come if you would like . . . You see, it is ze next stop.'

'*Oui, merci*,' giggled Ushi. 'Well . . .' she said to Stella and Jodie when François had left the carriage, 'what do you think?'

'Yeah, sounds ideal,' said Jodie. 'And no wonder *you* fancy it, Ush!'

'What d'*you* reckon Stell?' Ushi turned to her other friend, 'I mean we've all got to want to go there, haven't we? We agreed, remember? Before we came away? We said we'd be democratic. So what d'you think?'

'I'm er . . . I'm not . . .' began Stella doubtfully, but then she smiled. 'Oh, what the hell! Yeah, yeah – let's go for it – it sounds great.'

Ushi grinned. 'Doesn't it just?!!!'

Unspoilt the village certainly was. From what Ushi

could see, there was just one campsite, one hotel, one café/bar and a beach. But what a beach it was! It unfurled like a bright, broad, golden ribbon into the distance and was backed by dunes and lapped by a blue-green sea.

'You stay 'ere? *Oui*?' asked François. 'You like?'

'*Oui, oh oui*,' murmured Ushi, standing so close to him she could smell his cologne – kind of lemony and herby and distinctly foreign-smelling. 'And the resort isn't bad either.' Stella and Jodie, bless 'em, went to book in, leaving Ushi alone for a few minutes with François.

'You want we go to the beach this afternoon?' he asked.

'Sounds good,' said Ushi. 'Be a whole crowd of us, will it? You and your mates plus the three of us? Yeah, we could take picnic!'

'Oh . . .' Francois began hesitantly. 'We go in a crowd? *Je ne sais pas*. My friends . . . they may not be 'ere yet. I go to the campsite and see. I meet you on the beach, *n'est-ce pas*?' He bent forward to kiss her. After a moment's hesitation, Ushi responded. Mmmmm-hmmmm, he certainly knew how to use those pouty lips of his – and his tongue was pretty nifty, too. He obviously didn't believe in wasting any time. This was French kissing for real! His hands moved from her shoulder and started to roam her back – over her shirt – and then suddenly she felt his fingers tugging insistently at her bra strap.

Ushi pulled away. Crikey Moses, he was more than a bit cheeky. She'd only known him a few hours and here he was wanting to explore her underwear! Well, he could forget that. While it was true she fancied him, she rather than he would dictate the pace of things. And at the mo' – hardly knowing him – she wanted to go slow.

François was eyeing her speculatively.

'Down boy!' Ushi grinned.

'*Comment?*' said François.

Ushi shook her head. 'Forget it. We'll see you in an hour or so.'

'Ouch, ooch, ouch!' yelped Jodie as they walked across the sand some time later. 'It's boiling, isn't it? Like walking over burning coals. Oooh, I can't wait to get in the sea.'

'You want to be careful, Jodes, with your fair hair and complexion,' advised Stella. 'The sun really zaps people like you. Are you all oiled-up?'

'Yes Mum,' laughed Jodie. She looked around the beach. There were a few people about but no

François. 'He's not here yet then, Ush?'

Ushi stretched her arms above her head and shook back her hair. 'Doesn't look like it. Come on, let's go for it! Last one in the sea buys the ice creams.'

Yelling like banshees, they dumped their towels and bag full of newly bought French bread, cheese and fruit, and ran down to the sea. In spite of the heat of the day, the water felt freezing. Ushi gasped and squealed as she splashed about. She soon warmed up though. Lying on her back, staring up at the bluer-than-blue sky, she realised she was living the fantasy she'd played out in her mind, over and over again.

Stella nudged her suddenly. 'Hey up, lover boy's just arrived,' she said gesturing with her head towards the beach. She started giggling. 'You can tell he's French, can't you? An English lad would never dare to wear what he's got on. Oooh look at him preening! Fancies himself, doesn't he?'

Ushi stood up in the water and shielded her eyes to look towards the beach. She felt her lips twitching. Stella had a point but then so, it was very, very apparent, did François – dressed as he was in a pair of miniscule trunks. It was a blessing he had such a great body.

Jodie joined them. 'You going over to say hello then?' she asked.

'In a bit,' said Ushi. 'I haven't finished my swim yet.'

'He seems to be on his tod,' Jodie went on. 'What d'you want us to do? Leave you two love-birds alone for a bit?'

Ushi shook her head. 'God, no! We'll run out of stuff to say. And anyway, gorgeous he may be, but he knows it. I don't want be left alone with him. I told you how amorous he was earlier. Blimey! If it was just the two of us I bet he'd be trying to get me bikini off in seconds!'

'You can stay put, love,' hissed Stella out of the corner of her mouth. 'He's just dived in. Looks like the mountain's coming to Mohammed!'

Seconds later, François' sleek head bobbed up beside Ushi. She wanted to laugh. With his hair plastered down on either side of his head, he looked a bit like a sealion!

'Your friends not around then?' said Ushi.

'*Non.*' Francois shook his head. 'But they leave a message for me. They wait a little further up the beach. More – how-you-say – secluded. You want we should go there?'

Ushi quickly glanced at Stella and Jodie. Both

shrugged. They obviously didn't care one way or t'other. It was up to her. Yeah, why not?

'Er, OK,' she said. 'We're up for it.'

They seemed to have walked miles.

'God,' Stella gasped. 'I feel like I'm wandering across the Sahara. Where the hell are your mates, François?'

François, who was walking slightly ahead, turned. 'We find them soon, I'm sure.'

'Yeah, well can't we stop for a bit now?' said Jodie. 'Find 'em later? I'm burning up and I'm starving.'

'Yeah,' Ushi agreed. 'We want to stop.'

'OK,' shrugged François.

They sank down onto the sand. Jodie quickly put up the parasol while Stella and Ushi started sorting out the food.

'Would you like some . . .' The words stuck in Ushi's throat as she turned to François. 'Ohmigod!' she managed to squeak. 'Ohmigod! What *are* you doing?'

Stella's and Jodie's gasps added to Ushi's as François started to take off his trunks! He smiled at Ushi.

'There is a problem? I think not. *C'est une plage*

naturisme. Ze clothes are not allowed 'ere. I zink you will love it, Ushi. Be at one wiz the nature.'

'Not on your life,' Ushi muttered. 'You do what you like but I'm staying clothed, ta very much.'

François shrugged in a peculiarly Gallic way, stood up and without a backward glance at any of them, strolled leisurely towards the sea. They stared after him. Stella was the first to speak.

'Well . . .' she said. 'Your antennae were spot-on on this occasion Ush. You were right. If you'd been left alone with him, he *would* have tried to get that ikkle old bikini off that beautiful body of yours. What d'you wanna do now? Y'know, I don't know if I like this end of the beach all that much. I certainly don't fancy meeting whatsisface's mates – not here, anyway. I bet they'll all be starkers, too. Call me old-fashioned, but I like to know a person for a bit before they start stripping off in front of me.'

'Me too,' said Ushi.

Jodie suddenly started to giggle. 'There's a bloke and a woman hiding in the sand dunes,' she tittered. 'Neither of 'em have got a stitch on. She's dead skinny and he's a real podge. Ohmigod! It's disgusting!'

'Stop it, Jodes,' murmured Ushi but couldn't help having a sneaky look herself. 'I wanna get out of here. Preferably before François comes back. I don't think I'll be able to look him in the face for a start.'

She started laughing. Stella, too, while Jodie was still tittering away to herself.

'Come on, quick!' Ushi gasped, piling their picnic back into the bag. Next to a bottle of water lay François' discarded trunks. She almost stuffed them into the bag. He'd tricked her. If he'd told her that he was taking her to a naturist beach, she'd never have agreed to go. She should have sussed it when he'd gone on about this place being 'so very *naturel*'. To take or not to take his keks? That was the question. The thing was she much didn't fancy them being in close proximity to their food! And she didn't wish to be accused of theft.

'What are you doing?' asked Jodie as Ushi began to make a hole in the sand. 'It's hardly the right time to start building bloody sandcastles!'

'I'm not,' giggled Ushi. 'I'm hiding François's trunks. Trying to find them will give him something to do when he emerges from the sea. I mean, he won't have us gorgeous girlies to chat to anymore!'

'Ushi!' said Stella. 'Do you really think you should?'

Ushi swiftly piled sand onto the already partially buried garment. She stood up and smiled.

'Too late! I just have.'

Lazing around on the beach in front of their hotel, they kept a look-out for François all afternoon but to their disappointment, he didn't materialise.

'I wonder what he did when he couldn't find his teeny-weeny trunklets?' mused Jodie as they were packing up to leave.

'Made himself a new pair out of seaweed,' laughed Stella. 'Or maybe he found an old banana-skin lying around on the beach.'

'A bit of orange peel would have done just as well,' muttered Ushi.

'OOOO-er,' teased Jodie and Stella. 'Bitchy, bitchy!'

'Well . . .' Ushi grinned. 'It serves him right.'

Jodie suddenly gave a sharp intake of breath. 'Don't look now,' she gulped, 'but he's walking along the beach. With another bloke and a very coupley-looking couple. Must be his mates.'

Ushi froze. 'What's he wearing?' she hissed. 'Not the trunks?'

Jodie shook her head and literally started to shake with laughter.

'He's not still naked?' Stella squealed, not daring to look herself.

Jodie shook her head again. 'Ohmigod, he's leaving his mates and walking towards us . . .'

'Never mind that!' Ushi hissed again. 'Quick, tell us what he's wearing!'

'A . . .' began Jodie but then she stopped suddenly.

'Ushi?' It was François.

Steeling herself, Ushi looked round and literally had to bite her lip. He was wearing a woman's swimsuit pulled down to his waist. This would have looked daft enough in any instance but this particular cozzy just happened to have a fitted bra bit in the top and the underwired 'cups' were on obvious display, bobbing like unfettered buoys around his middle. He looked ridiculous.

'Oh, hi,' Ushi spluttered, trying with difficulty to keep her eyes trained on his face.

'What 'appen to you?' François asked. 'I return to the beach after my swim and you not there . . .'

'I wasn't feeling well,' Ushi replied with sudden inspiration. 'Too much bum, I mean, sun!'

'Oh,' François shrugged. 'I wonder if you see my swimming trouser. They too had gone when I came back from my swim. I wonder if . . .' he grinned,

'you bring them back wiz you. As a joke, *peut-être?*
Le souvenir, possiblement?'

Ushi shook her head, not trusting herself to speak.

'Don't flatter yourself, lad!' muttered Stella.

'*Peut-être* a dog nabbed 'em,' piped up Jodie.

François shrugged again. '*Peut-être. Alors . . .*
We meet later, Ushi? The two of us this time?
Oui?'

'*Non!*' Ushi shook her head and linked arms
with Jodie and Stella. She wasn't going anywhere
without her posse, especially now François had
revealed himself – literally – in his true colours.
'I'm a pack animal,' she said. 'Where I go, they
go. Sorry, but that's the way it is. Right girls?'

'*Absolument!*' agreed Stella and Jodie in unison.

'Well, girls?' said Ushi once François had gone.
'What's it to be tonight? I don't know about you
but after last night, I fancy an early one. 'Specially
as we're moving on tomorrow. All this seclusion is
fine and dandy but I think we want somewhere a
bit more happening, *n'est-ce pas?*'

Coincidentally, the first train out of the village the
next morning was going to St Marion. '*St Marion
. . .*' Ushi read out from her guide book once they

were settled aboard. '*An attractive resort that's had something of a facelift in recent years. As much a favourite with body-boarders and surf enthusiasts as it is with the more traditional holidaymaker, St Marion boasts wide, sandy beaches, chic little pavement cafés and is famed for her seafood.*' Ushi put down her book. 'So what do we think? A hit or a miss?'

'A hit,' said Stella. 'It sounds like the kind of place where there'll be loads going on – not a remote bloody naturist resort – thank God! The kind of place where we'll be happy to stop for a few days. I fancy that – I'm knackered with all this running around.'

'Me too,' said Jodie. 'I say we get to St Marion and completely chill out. I also say a hit! But let's make sure we get there this time. I don't care if some speci-men of spunkiness personified gets on this train and tries to talk us into going 'somewhere really special', we're bound for St Marion! Agreed, Ush?'

'Agreed,' Ushi smiled a tad guiltily. 'I sure like the sound of it. Body-boarders and surfers, eh? You know what that means, don't you!'

'Mmm-hmmm . . . !' Jodie and Stella nodded together.

'Totty!' Ushi went on. 'Hoardes of it, too. Groovy-looking guys in tighter-than-tight wetsuits.

So much sexier, in my opinion, than geezers in the altogether!'

'Well hallejuiah for that!' proclaimed Stella.

'Just you wait,' Ushi grinned. 'There'll be plenty of action going in a surf resort like St Marion. I've been to Cornwall, see. I know!'

St Marion station was bathed in sunshine as their train arrived two hours later. They clambered down onto the platform with their rucksacks and staggered out onto the concourse.

'Any ideas, guys?' asked Ushi.

'I guess it'll have to be a campsite, yeah?' said Jodie.

Stella nodded.

'You guys stay here with the bags and I'll go and sort it,' said Ushi. 'Won't be long.'

The tourist information officer recommended a campsite called *La Plage*. It certainly looked nice enough from the brochure he handed Ushi. There was a pool, tennis court, clubhouse, Bar-B-Q area and spotless-looking loos. And, as the name suggested, it was right on the beach. Ushi, after a quick consultation with Jodie and Stella, decided to book them in.

*

Through Ushi's Armani-type shades, the sun was a swirling orange ball set in an infinite purple sky. The sea looked to be practically the same shade – perhaps slightly more violet – tipped with creamy, white crests. And as for the sand? Ushi grabbed a handful. Slipping through her fingers, it felt like powdered silk and looked like powdered gold. She sighed and lay back on her beach towel. She'd already thought it before on this trip but this really was the life. And how could she ever have thought that she hated camping? Today, she loved it. The tent had gone up like a dream and their sleeping bags, now thoroughly dried out, were cosily positioned inside. Jodie, bless her, had even laid out their nighties on top of them and now Ushi was actually looking forward to snuggling down that evening. But that was hours away yet. In the meantime, there was loads more to look forward to. Checking out their fellow campers for a start. True there seemed to be a few famlies staying at *La Plage* but luckily most of the clientele seemed to be made up of young, free and single like themselves. She'd already noticed a number of likely-looking lads. No one who, as yet, could quite compare with freaky François in the looks department but, hell, after yesterday, she thought she'd preferred someone not quite so physically fanciable who'd keep their swimming cozzy on!

'I think we should stay here a few days to recharge our batteries,' Jodie piped up suddenly from the beach towel next to Ushi's. 'What d'you two think?'

'I don't want to think about anything,' murmured Ushi. 'I just want to lie back, empty my head of all thoughts and catch some rays.'

'I fancy an ice cream,' Stella announced suddenly and stood up. 'Anyone else?'

'I fancy a willing slave who'll massage me with sun cream,' sighed Ushi. 'But if you can't find one, I guess I'll make do with *une glace*, ta.'

She yawned, suddenly feeling very sleepy. All this lying around doing nothing was exhausting. She must have dropped off then because the next thing Ushi knew, she was being shaken awake by a worried-looking Jodie.

'It's Stella,' she muttered. 'She's gone.'

Ushi yawned and stretched. God, Jodes could be such a worrier at times.

'She'll have gone back to the tent,' said Ushi. 'You know what she's like – brain like a sieve at times. I bet she's forgotten all about our ice creams and gone back for a siesta.'

Jodie shook her head. 'She hasn't – I've looked.

I can't think what's happened to her.'

Ushi rolled onto her tummy and took off her shades to get a better look up the beach. It was filling up and she couldn't see Stella anywhere. She could see loads of talent, though. Just as she'd predicted. Oooooh yes, that guy presently walking up the beach in their direction . . . With his cropped blond hair and tanned, everso taut body, he really was something else. Problem was he was holding the hand of a rather lovely, tall, dark girl dressed in a rather lovely, pale-yellow bikini. Ushi sat up suddenly. She recognised that bikini! She ought to. It was hers. She'd lent it to Stella a few hours earlier. Well, well, well, lucky old Stell! With a lad like that in tow, no wonder she'd forgotten all about their ice creams.

'Here . . .' Ushi nudged Jodie who was busy scanning the sea for anyone who might look like Stella. 'You can stop worrying. Get a load of this! The wanderer has returned. Looks very much like Stella's gone and pulled.'

But before Jodie had chance to say anything, Stella and her new boy-babe were practically on top of them.

'Hi,' murmured Stella in a breathy whisper. 'This is Tomas.'

♥

Love Lines

Day Three

St Marion

Before we came away I promised myself I'd 'do' my diary every day. Great start huh? But we've been having such a ball, putting pen to paper is the last thing I've felt like doing. Been too busy living it up to want to sit down and reflect on it all. The red leather, oh all right, leather-look binding and all these snowy white pages are mocking me now, though, so I'd better get on with it. I want to call me travel tome something clever and timeless but at the moment I guess plain, old Stella's Diary will have to do.

Travelling around like this is just the best fun. I knew it would be, but it's even better than I imagined. Real independence for once – it's fantastic! Independence!!! I was dreading the ferry crossing a bit because I knew I'd chuck up but as we all did, it made it into a group activity somehow. Puking was a bonding experience! Taking the rise out of those stuck-up creeps was a good laugh, too. Hope we don't run into them again. I was dreading telling the girls about the Aunty Maria thing. I was just embarrassed really. I mean, Ushi's mum and stepdad are so cool and liberal about everything and Jodie's mum's quite together, too – though nowhere near as hip 'ngroovy as Ushi's folks. It's like "Hey great! Have a fab time. If it feels good, do it!" with them but mine still treat me like I'm just fresh outta nappies. Old-fashioned mother and old-fashioned, Spanish *father*? It's not the coolest, most laid-back parenting experience in the world. As it turned out though, Jodes and Ush were fine about it. It was probably a bit silly of me to think they wouldn't be – they're me best mates and know what my olds are like. I'm not quite sure how they'll react when we reach the Pyrenees and they realise that there really is *very* little to do, that it gets freezing cold at night, even in summer, and that Miguel's tons more nerdy than cute. But I'll worry about that later.

Yep, we're having a brilliant crack. The best ever. Looking back, even that first night at that crap campsite doesn't seem so bad. I keep having flashbacks of the three of us mooching about in the rain, unable to see what we're doing, snapping each other's heads off and I keep laughing to myself. Yesterday was a right laugh too – the 'so special, so naturel' resort. I thought there was something a bit creepy about François – it was why I wasn't exactly gagging to go to his undiscovered paradise. Maybe I'm being unfair. Maybe he genuinely thought we'd be into all that naturist stuff. Well, he got the wrong gals. Buzzy and happenin'; St Marion is much more 'us'. I just lurve it – especially since I met Tomas!

Tomas ... Ushi's right about foreign names. They're too damned sexy for their own good. Tomas is a world apart, though. The sexiest name out, I reckon – all exotic and romantic. Funny, I always thought German lads had names like Hans or Helmut. A complete turn off. 'Course it helps that this particular Tomas looks a like a bit of a star.

Forgive me dear diary while I totally indulge myself but the way I met him was like something out of a film – and I want to relive it over and over again. There I was, the leading lady, sauntering along the edge of the sea, wondering just when I was going to meet my leading man, when suddenly this surfer appeared from nowhere – on his board – and literally knocked me off my feet! I was none too pleased until it sank in just what this very apologetic surfer looked like – a bit of a sun god in a wet suit, as a matter of fact. I wasn't really hurt but I made out I was shaken up with the shock of it all so that he'd help me up. (I know, I know, but the old ones are always the best.) It worked like a dream! He picked me up – actually scooped me up in his arms, so romantic – and made all these sympathetic noises. Problem was, I couldn't work out what he was saying because it was all in German. He gently put me down and we stood there for ages just grinning at each other. I could tell he fancied me because he didn't let go of my hand and his blue eyes were sooo sparkly. Anyway, I reluctantly started walking back up the beach and he followed me. That was it really. We started walking together and having this weird conversation – unlike the rest of him, his English isn't too hot. It was all very 'me Tarzan, you Jane' sort of stuff but we managed to suss out each other's names. I was so into it all – or rather him – I had no idea where we were going and the next thing I knew, I was back where I'd started and we were practically on top of Ushi and Jodes!

I felt a bit bad 'cos I'd forgotten the ice creams but Jodie and Ushi didn't seem to care and just kept smirking knowingly across at Tomas and me.

I introduced Tomas to the girls but it was a bit difficult because neither of them speak German either. So after I'd given Jodes and Ush a quick rundown on how we'd met and told them that, no, I didn't yet know if he had any nice mates, the four of us sat around just grinning at each other with Ushi and Jodie occasionally giggling and whispering to each other.

Tomas kind of indicated that we go for a drink.

Ushi said to go for it, but I said no. It wasn't as if I thought Tomas was into bathing au naturel or anything like that, but after yesterday's hoo-haa, I didn't fancy being on my own with him just yet and the girls didn't fancy a drink. So I'm meeting him tonight instead. We all are – with Jodes and Ush hoping he's got some cute mates. He's bound to. What top lad like him wouldn't? And quelle coïncidence! *He just happens to be stopping at our campsite. Major piece-a-luck, eh?*

Tomas – looking hornier than any rhino – is waiting for us in the club house. Some guys have just got it, some guys haven't. Tomas has 'it' in skipfuls. He's an out and out love god as far as I'm concerned!

'Guten Abend,' he says in this deep, gutteral voice which I just know will bring out the animal in me. He takes my hand and I feel like I've just put my fingers in an electric socket. The zzzzzing is sooooo strong!

He seems to be on his own – I'm surprised – but I'll suss out his mate situation later. At the moment, I just too busy gazing into those brilliantly bright eyes.

Once we're sitting down with drinks, I can feel the rest of the world just melting away around me. I just want to be myself and let Tomas get to know the real me. It seems though that Jodes and Ushi are feeling a bit bored and have other plans . . .

'I just lurve this record!' Jodie proclaims as the antiquated juke-box in the corner starts up. 'I've just recorded it actually.'

She starts singing away. Tomas looks seriously confused. Ushi starts laughing and I start blushing. Can't Jodie see how stupid she looks – this is no time for playing alter egos. I know they feel left out of the action, but honestly! Fortunately Jodes gets the hint after a bit and shuts up.

The trouble is, I'd be happy to sit here all night and Tomas seems in no hurry to move. Unfortunately for me and Mr Love, the girls soon start getting restless. Can't blame 'em really. The club house is practically empty and with me and Tomas doing the 'eye-magnet' and pigeon English/ German, they're a bit bored.

'Have you, er, asked him about his mates?' asks Ushi when he's gone to the loo. 'Or who he's here with? Couldn't we, er, join them? I mean there's not much here for me and Jodes to do, is there?'

She's right so when Tomas gets back, I kind of indicate that we want to go.

'Your friends?' I say. 'We go to them?'

'O ja,' Tomas replies after a moment. 'OK.'

Jodie gets up so quickly, her chair goes flying. 'So what are we waiting for?' she grins.

We end up at this little bar called Le Poisson *(The Fish) on the other side of the bay. It takes over half-an-hour to get there and Jodes and Ush start complaining about being knackered. It's different for me. With Tomas's arm snaked around my waist, I feel like I could go on walking forever. In fact, I'm feeling more than just a bit light-headed and* shaky around the knees. We were about halfway there when Tomas stopped me suddenly and kissed me. As far as I'm concerned you can forget French kissing 'cos the Germans have got it licked. This particular German, anyway. He could snog for Germany! It went on for ages – and would probably still be going on now – if Ushi and Jodie hadn't eventually caught up with us and started making irritating kissy-kissy noises behind our backs.

Le Poisson doesn't look much from the outside but inside it's brilliant. The music's good and the crowd look pretty happenin' too. Fairly mixed with the odd semi-trendy wrinkly popping up here and there.

'Better late than never,' I yell to Ush and Jodes as we push our way through the bar, following Tomas. They give me a big smile but their expressions freeze when they see who Tomas has stopped in front of – and I must admit I'm a bit stunned, too.

The two men look fairly well-preserved in their denim shirts and chinos but there's no getting away from the fact that they are seriously ancient. They're old enough to be our dads at least which, looking back, should have given me a clue as to who exactly they are.

'Mein Onkel und mein Vater!' *announces Tomas, looking a bit sheepish. I see Jodie and Ushi exchanging glances and I know what's coming next. I'm right. The two of them start giggling hysterically.*

Tomas and his dad and uncle look at them like they're bonkers so I mutter an apology and drag them over to the other side of the bar.

'Jodes fancies his dad and I'll cop off with his Onkel,' splutters Ushi.

'No, I want Onkel!' snorts Jodie.

I bit my cheek to stop myself from laughing. If it wasn't for Tomas, I'd be shrieking away with them both. But then if it wasn't for Tomas, we wouldn't be here in the first place. 'Shhhh!' I hiss. 'Everyone's looking.'

Still spluttering slightly, Ush and Jodes take deep breaths and calm themselves down. Then Tomas comes over. He looks a bit hurt and I feel really bad. He obviously thinks we've been taking the piss. I look beseechingly at Ush and Jodie.

''SOK,' says Jodie. 'Don't you worry yourself, pet. It was just a surprise for us that's all. You know what we're like. We always laugh when we're nervous.'

'Yeah,' agrees Ush. 'Take yourselves off into a corner and do the sweet nothings bit.' She gazes

round the bar. 'There's loads of talent here. We'll be fine.'

I watch them both throw themselves into the fray, then gaze up at Tomas. He kisses me for a nanosecond but that's enough to turn me to jelly. I want to go on kissing him for ever. He smiles and takes my hand and I entwine my fingers with his. It sounds silly because we can't even have a proper conversation with each other but I really think I might be falling for him!

Day Five

Breakfasting Al Fresco at La Plage

There's no might about it! I am one fallen woman! Since that evening at Le Poisson, Tomas and me have been practically inseparable. We spend our days on the beach – Tomas is teaching me to surf and says I look wunderbar in a wetsuit – and most nights there, too. Last night – or rather very, very early this morning – I didn't get back till two. My mum and dad would freak if they knew. But Tomas is just the best kisser! Usually slow and unhurried, even lazy, when we start off but once he gets going, he gets really passionate. Just thinking about his kissing makes me want more. Lots more. He's really demonstrative, too, which makes a real change from the British lads I know, who can be dead off-hand. He's always kissing and hugging me – even when his rellies are about. Normally I'd be dead embarrassed but Tomas's uncle and dad (his parents are divorced) are so cool and continental about it, it doesn't bother me.

Unbelievably, Jodes and Ushi are having just as good a time as me. Actually, I'll adjust that – they're having almost as good a time as me. They've pulled, too. Ushi's hooked up with a lad called Biff – so much for sexy names but then he is a Brit – whom she met at Le Poisson that first night. He's mad about her, absolutely batty, which doesn't exactly displease Ush. She likes having her ego stroked does our Ush, but then don't we all? Facially, Biff's not that fab but being a surfer, he's got the most unbelievable bod on him. He's also dead funny and a nice bloke to boot. Jodie started slowly but she's made up for it over the last few days. She copped off with 'Bernie from Belgium' then she dumped him after a day – she says he stank of chips and mayo – then got together with a hunky French lad called Jean-Louis. They've been together ever since.

Anyway . . . I've decided I want to stay here forever! Oh all right, another week at least. It's just soooo, soooo perfect. There's the beach, great weather, a nice campsite, a happening after-dark scene and for me, of course, Tomas. What more could a girl want?

Day Seven

La Plage *Café-Bar*

It's started to rain today but that's not the only reason I'm feeling like hacked off and as miserable as sin. Funny how quickly things change. Forty-five minutes ago, I was the happiest little soul in St Marion. I was sitting here, at the table I'm still sitting at, having brekkie with Ushi – Tomas had gone off fishing with his dad (I declined cos of my seasickness) – when Jodie walked in, waving this leaflet around in her hand.

'Take a look at this,' she said. 'I've just seen it. It sounds brilliant. Really amazing. I'm desperate to go.'

It was a flyer for a music festival – kind of like a French Glastonbury – with loads of bands including the fantastic 'Divali', performance artists, dance tents, alternative therapies and the like. She was right. I thought it sounded fab, too.

'Count me in,' I said, before I realised that the festival was happening near Bordeaux, miles and miles away down the coast.

''SOK,' Ushi said when I pointed this out. 'Jodes and me were only saying last night that it was about time we moved on. We've been here five days and the weather's gone off on us. We may as well pack up and leave today. Won't take long. In fact, if we want to make this festival at all we're going to have to. It's only on for two days and it starts tomorrow. Plus it's a set price so we want to get our money's worth.'

I was thrown into a complete state of panic. I didn't want to leave Tomas. Not yet.

'What about Biff?' I said to Ushi. 'You can't leave him, Ush.'

She looked at me as if I'd lost my mind. 'Course I can,' she laughed. 'Biff and me have had a good crack but that's all. He's nice enough to have spent a few days with and wile away the time while you've been joined at the hip to Tomas but all good things and all that. Blimey, I probably wouldn't even have looked at Biff at home. He's not really my type.'

I turned to Jodie. 'Jean Louis . . .' I said. 'You've only just met him. Wouldn't you like to spend more time with him?'

Jodie shook her head. 'Not really. Certainly not if it means missing out on this festival, no. And like Ushi, me feet are getting a bit itchy. The old batteries are recharged and it's time we explored pastures new.'

I couldn't help myself. I just burst into tears. 'I don't want to go,' I sobbed. 'I don't want to.'

'You don't want to leave Tomas,' said Ushi gently and put her arm around me. 'But you're going to have to, Stell. You knew you would, at some point. We can't stay here forever – we gotta get going. Hit the road again. There's so much more to see and experience.' She grinned and nudged me. 'Like loads more lads . . .'

'I don't want anyone else,' I muttered.

Jodes and Ushi looked at each other.

'It's time, Stell,' said Jodie. 'Really. In fact I'm, er, going to start taking the tent down. We'd better leave soon – the sooner the better, in fact. We want to get to Bordeaux as early as poss. Then we'll get ourselves a decent camping spot – that's if there's any left.'

As early as poss . . . This gives me hardly any time

to say goodbye – if at all. Tomas probably won't be back from fishing till mid-afternoon. When I mention this to Jodie and Ushi, they say they're real sorry but there's nothing to be done and I'll have to leave him a letter. A letter, for God's sake? I can't say what I want to say in a letter. Can't even kiss him goodbye.

'Stella, we can't hang around till then,' says Ushi. 'I mean, he might not even get back till this evening which will mean us missing a huge chunk of the festival altogether. It finishes tomorrow, remember.'

But suddenly I don't care if I miss it. I just don't care about anything except Tomas.

To The Max

'Where does Ivor the Engine live?' asked Ushi.

'Er . . . dunno,' said Jodie.

'Rails!' Ushi grinned. 'Your turn, Jodes.'

Jodie had one ready. 'What did the big engine say to the little engine?'

Ushi shook her head.

'Time you started training!' Jodie was suddenly inspired. 'You'll like this one too. Why do train drivers wear specs?' She didn't wait for Ushi to even hazard a guess. 'Because they've got tunnel vision!'

Ushi groaned, shaking her head. 'That's terrible!'

Jodie nudged Stella. 'Your go.'

Moving as if she was in slow motion, Stella turned to look at Jodie. She'd been staring morosely out of the window ever since they'd boarded the train.

'Your go, Stella,' Jodie repeated.

Stella shook her head. 'I'm not in the mood,' she muttered and started staring out of the window again.

Jodie started to say something – along the lines that Tomas apart, there was still loads more to look forward to – but she changed her mind. It probably wouldn't do any good anyway. She couldn't help feeling a smidge guilty. Had she and Ushi been out of order about wanting to leave St Marion? OK, it had been a spur-of-the-moment thing but when they'd been discussing the kind of holiday they'd all wanted before they'd come away, all three of them had agreed that spontaneity would be one of the best things about a trip like this.

It would, Jodie decided, have been pretty rough on Stella if she hadn't been able to see Tomas before they'd left. But she had. He'd come back from his fishing trip earlier than expected because of the crap weather and she'd been able to spend a bit of time with him.

'Not long enough to say goodbye properly,' Stella had moaned, but Jodie reckoned she'd have said that even if she and 'Testosterone Tomas', as Jodie and Ushi had secretly christened him, had had a couple of hours to make their fond farewells.

Fair do's, they'd had five days at St Marion.

Fun days they'd been, too. But now it was time to move on – especially for something as exciting as this festival in Bordeaux. Events like this hardly happened every day, and she couldn't wait.

True enough, Jean-Louis had been hot stuff, but Europe, she was delightfully discovering, was full of them. And anyway, what was the point of putting all your eggs in one basket when there were oodles more pebbles on the beach.

Well, if Stella wasn't going to play ball, it was Ush to go again.

'Your joke, I think, Ush,' Jodie said.

'Nah.' Ushi shook her head. 'I can't think of any more.'

Jodie watched as Ushi moved closer to Stella, grabbed hold of her hand and squeezed it. Jodie couldn't help feeling relieved. Yeah, she'd leave the tea-and-sympathy bit to Ushi. Ushi always seemed to know what to say at times like this. Hopefully, she'd make Stella snap out of her depressing mood. It was spoiling the prospect of the festival for all of them. Besides, it wasn't good for Stella to sit and brood over a guy. Life – and in particular this trip – was too short. She'd have a good few days she'd always remember. Time now for something different. Something which promised to be even better!

'It was time to go, Stell,' Ushi said quietly. 'Apart from anything else, I know what you're like. In a day or two, you would have been sick of him, anyway.'

'I wouldn't,' Stella replied, defensively.

'Oh no?' Ushi questioned. 'Come on, you're like it at home. You were wild about Matthew for about a week and then you went off him. It was the same with that Paul lad and that Irish student your mum had to stop last summer. You're hot for 'em one minute but the next . . .' she clicked her fingers, 'you cool right down. You get bored when they're over keen. It would have been the same with Tomas. Go on, admit it. Be honest with yourself.'

'I am being,' Stella insisted. 'I don't think it would have been like that with Tomas. He . . .' She shook her head. 'Oh, I don't know . . . Maybe if I'm totally honest, he was starting to get on my nerves a tiny bit. He was dead clingy at times. I could barely go to the loo without him wanting to come with me.'

'I know what you mean,' Ushi nodded in agreement. 'Biff was a bit like it, too. That kind of attention's nice enough but, boy, can it get claustrophobic! So many boys, when you get to know 'em, are like it, too.' Her eyes went all dreamy.

'Davy's different, though. He seems to be able to tap into my subconscious. It's like telepathy. He knows when I'm in a demonstrative kind of mood and when I want leaving alone. He's sensitive like that.'

'Tomas was sensitive . . .' considered Stella. 'But sometimes he . . .'

Jodie looked out of the window. She wasn't in the mood for this kind of retrospective boy talk. She suddenly felt super-energetic and wanted to get out there. It had stopped drizzling and the flat fields of northern France were eons away from the rolling countryside of western France. It was exciting, dramatic and exhilarating and Jodie immediately had the most fabulous feeling that Bordeaux would be all of those things for her, too.

While she'd been on the train, Jodie had wondered if, once in Bordeaux, it would be hard trying to find out where the festival was happening. The directions on the flyer were pretty sketchy. But she needn't have worried. On leaving the station, they'd simply followed the snake-like procession of like-minded souls, the mile or so out of town to the site.

It was bigger than Jodie had expected and had

a kind of surreal quality. In many ways, this temporary canvas town seemed far more vibrant than the ancient, permanent one it bordered. And it was odd to think that, in another few days, there'd be nothing here but green fields again.

'Life's a pitch!' Ushi quipped, as they put up their tent. She shielded her eyes against the afternoon sunshine and looked around. 'Hey, this site's filling up really quickly. Good job we left when we did or we wouldn't have made it. And thank God we did make it because you know something? I think – no, I can feel – this festival is going to be dead cool.'

Jodie shivered suddenly. She was experiencing it again. The sensation she'd had on the train. A feeling that anything was possible here and that maybe even a life changing experience was in the offing – or at least a seriously life enhancing one. This was her first music festival. In previous years, she'd been desperate to go to one at home but her mum had always said she was too young. No longer, though. Mum was miles away. The shackles of home had been liberated. She could do whatever she wanted and, at this moment, she felt that 'whatever' was more than possible here. It felt almost essential.

Ushi had evidently imbibed the vibe and even Stella looked a smidge more cheerful as Jodie watched her taking it all in.

'Not exactly the Girl Guides, is it?' she muttered as a rather freaky looking couple walked past arm-in-arm.

'And this is only the camping ground!' Jodie laughed. 'Just think what it's like inside the arena.'

Ushi suddenly made a weird howling sound, as her hips gyrated to the bass-heavy music coming from the festival area, proper.

'Into the arena, my darlings!' she announced spookily. 'The hour is nigh!'

The arena was, thought Jodie, in many ways rather how she imagined a medieval village to be – mixed with '60s psychedelia. There were wonderful-smelling food stalls, groovy clothes stalls, artsy craft stalls, palmistry stalls, crystal stalls . . . and all the while, this constant backbeat of thumping, rhythmic music.

She loved it – every part of it. She'd never been anywhere like it before and she wanted to explore every inch of it. Trouble was, there was so much to experience it was hard to know where to start. In the end, Ushi made the decision for her.

'I'm hungry,' she moaned. 'I need sustenance. Breakfast was hours ago and we missed lunch.'

All three of them decided on curry. They were standing next to a stall which was giving off some truly divine, coriander and cumin scented aromas.

'Hey, it's from Bradford,' said Jodie, spotting the sign above the stall. 'Even better. The French may be clever at your fancy foreign stuff but nobody can do a Ruby like we can.'

'Yeah,' agreed Ushi. 'And I bet most of the customers are curry-starved Brits.'

Jodie had just been handed a steaming plate of vegetable korma when she began to wish that they'd opted for some other cuisine-of-the-world instead. Vietnamese, perhaps. Or kebabs. But it had nothing to do with the food. Rather the braying laugh coming from the queue behind them. She gave a furtive glance back before nudging Ushi.

'What did you say about curry-starved Brits? It's only Smarm-Features and mates from the ferry! Ohmigod! What shall we do?'

Ushi glanced back.

'Too late to do anything,' she muttered. 'We've been spotted.'

'Ah, the lovely laydeez we met on the high seas,' Smarm smarmed as he and his two mates caught up with them. 'We meet again. I was hoping we would. Hey, we've been missing ya! *N'est-ce pas mes amis?*'

'Give it a rest, Piers,' said one of his friends. 'Your French is shocking. Hi girls,' he grinned at all of three of them but his eyes were, Jodie noticed, firmly fixed on Ushi. So he fancied Ush! Well, lucky old her. Seeing him close-up, Jodie reflected that he looked a bit like a ferret. 'Didn't get a chance to introduce myself before. I'm Dominic but my friends call me Dom.'

The third member of the trinity then promptly introduced himself. 'The name's Flyte. Richard Flyte.'

'That cockney rhyming slang is it?' Stella suddenly piped up. 'You know – porkpies, lies; apple and pears, stairs; Richard Flyte, Mega-Tight.'

She didn't wait for him to reply but launched another blistering attack.

'Hey, you're not forking out for the scoff, are you? You'd better take care when you open your wallet or the months'll fly out! These curries don't come cheap y'know. Be at least double what those juices on the ferry cost.'

Jodie and Ushi started to laugh. By the sounds of it, Stella was back on form. Her jibe was right on target as Mega-Tight came over all defensive.

'I simply like value for money that's all,' he said. 'I don't like being taken for granted. I'm hardly destitute, sweetheart. I work in the city as a matter of fact. We all do.'

'Fascinating,' breathed Stella in serious sarcasm mode. They needed to get rid of these losers big-time, before anybody saw them with them, put two and two together and decided they were actually with these jerks!

Jodie was just thinking the same thing. As if Dom and Mega-Tight weren't bad enough, it was obvious who had the hots for her . . . Smarm-Features – wouldn't you just know it?

'What do you do?' he asked Jodie, standing so close to her she could smell his non-too-savoury beer breath.

'I'm a dental hygienist,' Jodie came back with, solemnly. 'Specialising in halitosis.'

'Hali . . . ?' Pukey Piers looked confused. Thick as well as seriously smarm-like. Not, Jodie decided, a winning combination.

'Bad breath,' she said pointedly and stared at him.

He looked at her warily then, deciding she had to be joking, started to laugh.

Jodie sighed. It was time, she felt, to take their

leave. This lot were seriously sad and if they didn't put a stop to it now, they'd never be able to shake them off. She glanced quickly at Ushi and Stella who were quick to follow her lead.

'We're off now,' yawned Ushi, pretending to drop off as Dom launched into a fascinating speech on the joys of off-shore investment.

'But we'd like to buy you laydeez a drink,' said Puke-Features. 'Now how about that? A glass of vino, yah?'

'Vino's strictly for toffs, isn't it?' quipped Stella. 'And we hate toffs . . .'

And with that final put-down they turned and started to walk away.

'God what a bunch of jerks,' breathed Stella. 'Do you think they've finally got the message, or what?'

They looked at each other and laughed. This holiday really was the best thing ever, Stella reflected as they walked on in companiable silence. And this festival was amazing, so many sights and sounds assailed her senses she felt almost dizzy with excitement as they lost themselves in the crowd.

'Not still missing old Tomas then, Stell?' Ushi asked eventually.

'No,' Stella sighed. 'In retrospect, I guess I've had

enough of the intensive-eyeball-gazing for a bit,' she laughed. 'So, what's next?'

They looked at each other and the same thought popped into each mind at the same time – shopping!

They browsed around the stalls. Stella bought some patchouli oil, Ushi a hippyish skirt and Jodie a tape. Then they gorged themselves on a bag of cookies from one of the food stalls before having a mad hour in one of the dance tents. It was dark when they emerged but there was still time to kill before 'Divali' came on stage.

'Back to the tent for a quick kip?' suggested Stella. 'I'm knackered now.'

But Jodie knew if they did that, they'd most likely flake out altogether and miss the rest of the evening. She suddenly had a brainwave. 'Massage!' she announced.

The other two looked at her, mystified.

'There's a holistic massage tent here somewhere,' she went on. 'I read about it. I really fancy that. You simply lie down and someone soothes away your aches and pains.'

'Ooo, I hope he's nice,' said Ushi.

'It's not necessarily a "he" who massages you,' said Jodie.

'Don't fancy it then,' shrugged Ushi. 'I'll come and watch, though.'

Shining their torches through the crowds, they eventually found the massage tent – having taken a wrong turning and spent a memorable and smelly five minutes in the gents' loos.

'Aren't you coming in, then?' asked Jodie, seeing Ushi and Stella starting to make themselves comfy on the ground.

'Changed me mind,' yawned Ushi. 'I fancy having a kip, too.'

'Just wake us up when you come out,' sighed Stella. 'Happy massage!'

Not really knowing why, Jodie felt a bit nervous as she walked into the large tent. Softly lit and delicately perfumed from a profusion of oil burners, tinkly new-age music was playing inside the tent giving it a mystical, serene feel. Several comatose-like punters lay spread out on the matting floor, being attended to by the masseures.

'Er, I'd like a massage please,' Jodie muttered in French to one of the off-duty masseuses, a girl who didn't look much older than Jodie.

'Non, non, je suis étudiante,' the girl said. 'Un moment, s'il vous plaît.'

She went behind a screen and a moment later

emerged, now accompanied by a guy of around the same age. 'This is Max,' she said in charming-accented English. 'He is trained masseur. He is very good.'

Jodie didn't know about that, but there was, she decided, something about Max that was very, very sexy. He wasn't chunky like Jean-Louis, wasn't in-yer-face gorgeous either. But he had the most adorable puppy-dog eyes and a fantastic smile that made her feel all gooey inside.

'Hi,' he said. 'You're English, right? Me too.'

Feeling even more nervous – but intensely excited – now she knew just whose fingers would be soothing away her aches and pains, Jodie lay down on the mat.

'Just relax,' Max whispered to her. 'The massage will last almost half-an-hour. OK?'

'OK,' Jodie whispered back and instantly wished it would be the longest half-hour ever. It was absolute bliss as those seemingly magic fingers of his attended to her neck, her shoulders, her head, her lower arms and legs and her feet. Jodie's heart was in her mouth. She'd never felt anything like it before in her life. Every time Max's fingers touched her skin it was like an electric current racing through her body. It had been a half-hour ride to heaven and by the time Max gently touched her on the elbow and told her the time was up she was like putty in his hands

'How was it?' he asked, helping her to her feet. 'Good?'

'Mmmmm.' Jodie smiled dreamily at him. She felt like she was floating. 'It was wonderful.'

'My pleasure.' He smiled back and seemed about to say something, then he hesitated.

'Yes?' asked Jodie. She momentarily wondered if she was being a bit forward but decided she didn't care.

Max smiled again and Jodie's insides did a series of gymnastic moves.

'We're shutting up the massage tent now. "Divali" are due on in a minute,' he said. 'Have you heard of them?'

Jodie laughed. 'Course she had. They just happened to be the best band going right now and one of the reasons she'd been so up for coming to the festival in the first place.

'Yeah, well . . .' Max went on, suddenly looking a bit shy. 'My brother's the singer and I was wondering if you would like to come and watch them with me. Backstage, I mean.'

Jodie literally pinched herself. This couldn't be

happening. It was a dream – it had to be. A gorgeous, sexy boy who just happened to be the brother of the singer in the most happening band in the world had asked her to go backstage with him, in the VIP area no less, where she'd no doubt be rubbing shoulders with no end of glam celebs and stars. This was too much! But, as she'd pinched herself to make sure, this was no dream.

'I'd love to,' she gulped, 'but I'd better tell my friends.'

He nodded. 'Be quick though, won't you? Security's really strict about letting people backstage once the band are on. And,' he looked embarrassed, 'I'm really sorry, but, I've er, only got two passes. Will your mates mind?'

'No problem,' gasped Jodie, 'leave it with me,' and she ran out of the massage marquee to find the others. How fantastic that he wanted to give his spare pass to her! Ushi and Stella surely wouldn't mind. How could they? This was a once-in-a-lifetime opportunity.

She circled the area around the tent but couldn't see them anywhere. They'd obviously moved but she knew they couldn't be too far away. Probably gone looking for food, if she knew Ushi. Should she look for them? 'Yes,' said her head. But her excitement gene said no. It might take ages and Max might be forced to go backstage without her. That, she didn't want to risk.

'But what if they worry?' Jodie argued with herself.

'They won't,' she argued back. 'They'll be cool. Stella and Ush aren't the worriers. You are.'

She ran back towards the massage tent, feeling even more like she was floating. When she got there, she couldn't see Max and thought for a moment he'd gone. She felt sick to the stomach. Shit! She'd missed him. But then she spotted him, standing at another entrance, waiting for her.

♥ French Letters

Dear Mum and Mark

Greetings from somewhere in south west France! We've been been gone for nine or ten days now – I'm losing track of time – so I thought I'd better write you to let you know I'm still alive. I actually bought a postcard to send you but I've decided to write a letter because we're having the best time ever and I've just got so much to tell. I'm enclosing the card anyway because I love the picture on the front – three old women in trad French cozzies. Guess who in 30 years time?

Sorry about my scrawl by the way – I've just noticed that my handwriting looks like a spiders' convention. It's not that the train's rickety – this is France after all and one thing the SNCF trains are not, is rickety – rather that I'm absolutely knackered because

I hardly got any sleep the night before last and it's just starting to catch up with me.

Why I didn't catch sufficient z's leads me very nicely into the most sensational thing that's happened to any of us so far on this trip. You'd better get yourself sat down for this, Mum, 'cos it's one helluva story. I could come straight out and tell you the punch line but for maximum dramatic effect – and I know you love a bit of drama – I'll start at the very beginning.

The day before yesterday, we arrived at this amazing music festival in Bordeaux. That's kind of in the last third of France nearest the Med and ... Oh I can't be bothered to explain. Go and get the atlas out of my bedroom. Got it? Found the map of France? Great! Bordeaux's on the Atlantic coast – sort of. Found it? Hurrah! Anyway, there we were at this festival ... Mark, you'd have loved it, you old hippy you. It was all incense, freaky music and loads of Jimi Hendrix looky-likies. Yep, you'd have fitted in well. Anyway, at around 8 pm on the first night, we were stand-ing outside this tent where they do massage 'cos Jodie wanted one. Me and Stella weren't into it so we had a bit of a rest while we were waiting for her. We were starving so we went on a food rekkie after about 20 minutes. We thought we'd only be a few minutes but it took ages – queues everywhere. Anyway, we eventually got back to the tent, having scoffed a revolting burger apiece, and couldn't find Jodie anywhere. Not only that, the massage tent was in darkness. Everyone had gone. We hung around for a bit but still no Jodie. Stella and me were a bit surprised she hadn't waited for us but we figured she must either have gone looking for us or been so relaxed by the massage, she'd drifted back to the tent for a snooze. At this point, we weren't too concerned – she had a torch and knew the way back to the campsite . . . God, Mum, I've just thought. Don't tell Jodie's mum this bit if you happen to bump into her. She'll freak out and say we should have gone looking for her straight away. We didn't think there was any need, though. Not at that stage. Anyway, we watched the main act and then headed back to the campsite, both of us half-thinking that we'd get back to the tent and find Jodie snuggled up inside. But she wasn't.

'Oh well,' we said to each other. 'She'll be here in a minute.' Half-an-hour went by and no Jodie. I started to feel a bit nervous but didn't say as much to Stella 'cos she was still acting like everything's fine and kept saying that Jodie would turn up any minute. But when another 10 minutes went by and she still hadn't showed up, we suddenly confessed to each other that we were worried sick. Anything could have happened to her. I kept imagining all these headlines in the papers at home: 'Young Traveller found Strangled at French Festival'. Stella reckoned Jodie might have gone off with these creeps we initially met on the ferry and bumped into again at the festival. But I doubted that very much.

We rushed back to security in the main arena and had real problems getting in 'cos the gates were locked and the guard spoke very little English. Eventually we managed to make ourselves understood, though. The head security guy, who fortunately did speak English, said the only thing he could do was put out a message on the tannoy. But he was a bit reluctant because he said it was late and, anyway, Jodie would probably be at the tent when we got back. At this point Stella completely lost it. She started screaming that if he didn't put out a message immediately she was going to squat in the HQ. She wasn't going to move until something was done. A message was duly put out, in French and English, appealing for Jodie to return to our tent or to get in touch with security, pronto. All we could do at this stage, old Security Trousers said, was wait for her. If she still wasn't back by morning, they'd put out more messages and, if necessary, organise a search party. Both Stella and I really started to freak when he said this. It was like one of those situations you read about, you dread, but you never think will happen to you. We were just about to leave, having given the most comprehensive description of Jodie we were able to under the circumstances, when his mobile phone suddenly rang. Backstage were calling because they'd heard the message. Apparently, Jodie was in the VIP area at a party!!! Can you believe that? We couldn't. Our ikkle Jodes hanging out with the rich and famous? No way! In fact, we were so sure it was a mistake, we demanded proof.

Security Trousers fiddled about with this close circuit video monitor, and the backstage area where the party was happening came up on screen. All these VIPs – mostly French but a few Brit stars as well – were standing around quaffing champagne. And there, in the middle of it all, stood Jodie and some other bloke – chatting and laughing with the lead singer of the headlining band – 'Divali', no less! Stella and I were so shocked, we literally couldn't speak. I eventually managed to ask if we could go and get her but Security Trousers said 'non'. The party was invite only and we hadn't been invited. There was nothing for me and Stella to do except go back to the tent and wait for the party animal to come back.

Sorry Mum. But I'm going to have to finish this later. I've written so much my hand feels like it's going to drop off. Stay tuned . . .

Ushi looked up from her letter to see Jodie, seated across the aisle of the train, smiling at her slightly quizzically.

'That's a long, long letter,' Jodie said. 'Who's it to?'

Ushi tapped her nose. 'You're not the only secretive one, you know. It's for me to know and you to find out.'

'We'll do a deal with you, Jodie,' said Stella, putting down her book. 'You tell us exactly what you got up to with the divine Max and Ushi'll tell you who she's written to. She'll even let you read the letter. Right, Ushi?'

Ushi nodded. 'Absolutely. If she spills.'

Jodie laughed. 'No thanks. Anyway, I think I probably already know what's in the letter. It's mostly about me, isn't it? You've been giving me furtive little looks all the time you've been writing it, so it must be.'

'Oh all right,' Ushi conceded. 'Yeah, it's mostly about you.'

'Ushi!' Stella scolded her. 'You're crap! You shouldn't have given in so easily.'

'There wasn't much point holding out,' muttered Ushi. 'It's hardly a fair exchange, is it? I let Jodie read my letter which'll tell her nothing new and she tells us all the juicy stuff about her glamorous new boyfriend.'

'He's not my boyfriend – not really,' sighed Jodie. 'It was a . . . a brief "holiday" encounter.'

'But pretty intense, huh?' asked Ushi.

What a dumb question, she thought, as soon as she'd said it. 'Course it had been intense. Intensely intense. Ushi still couldn't believe it. That Jodie had copped off with a geezer whose brother just happened to be the lead singer in 'Divali'. And he'd turned out to be more than just a one – very late – night stand. Jodie had arrived back at the tent at around 2 am that first night and then spent practically the whole of the next day – and night – with Max. They'd met him for a few minutes but that hadn't been nearly long enough to form much of an opinion. It had been fairly obvious that Jodie and he wanted to be alone, though.

She and Stella had started day two of the festival on their tods. The day itself wasn't that eventful – more shopping, more dancing, lots of wondering what Jodie was getting up to – but the evening had more than made up for it. They'd met up with a mad Irish gang – a few girls but mostly boys – shared a few bottles with them and ended up playing a frenzied game of 'Spin the Bottle'. Stella had kissed a couple of the guys but she, Ushi, had gone on a bit of a snog fest. In particular with one bloke, called Rory. It had all kind of fizzled out once the game was over, though, and at the end of the night she and Stella had stumbled back to the campsite to find the tent minus Jodie again. But, unlike last night, they'd both known where she was – or rather who she was with. They'd intended to stay awake so that they could interrogate her when she got back but had fallen asleep within a few minutes. Then Ushi woke up around 5 am to see Jodie climbing into her sleeping bag.

'Dirty stop out!' Ushi had whispered. 'Where've you been you bad lass?'

But Jodie had just put her finger to her lips, closed her eyes, and gone straight to sleep.

Ushi had asked the same question again this morning – several times. Stella too. But Jodie was giving nothing away. Something had happened. Something major. Why else would Jodie be being so secretive about Max? She'd given 'em the lowdown on the showbiz party but she'd hardly mentioned the Max Factor at all besides saying that yes, she had spent the day – and presumably most of the night – with him, too. And why, and this was the most interesting bit as far as Ushi was concerned, why was she going round glowing like a candle that was permanently aflame?

'Lurve,' Stella had said with certainty. 'Our Jodie's been out late a-lovin'.'

And Ushi thought she might be right. They wanted, they demanded, details. Jodie, however, was having none of it. Her lips, it seemed, were sealed. Well not for much longer. Unless Jodes started to dish – and soon – Ushi thought Stella and she would literally go potty. And what better way to wile away the train journey between Bordeaux and Toulouse – their next port of call – than with some extra juicy gossip? The problem was getting her to open up a tad. The best way, Ushi decided, was to be just a bit sneaky.

'You know, we really were worried about you the other night, Jodes,' Ushi began. 'I thought something terrible had happened to you.'

Jodie smiled regretfully, but Ushi could tell she was thinking 'Here we go again'. And Jodie couldn't blame her, she and Stella had really laid into her when she'd eventually arrived back at the tent on that first night, and again the next morning.

'I know,' sighed Jodie. 'And I'm sorry. I should have found you and told you where I was going – especially as I freaked out when each of you went missing for a bit. But don't you think I've said sorry enough now? Surely I'm forgiven.'

'You might be,' said Ushi. 'It depends.'

'On what?' Jodie began. Suddenly her eyes narrowed and she started to laugh. 'Oh I get it. This another of your "deals", is it? I'm only forgiven, you'll only stop going on about it, if I dish on Max and me. Am I right?'

Neither Stella nor Ushi spoke.

'I am,' Jodie went on. 'Aren't I?'

'Might be,' muttered Ushi eventually. There was no way Jodie would reveal anything now.

'Well, he first kissed me while we were at the party backstage,' said Jodie, quite conversationally – she could have been talking about the weather. 'I'd being dying for him to – all the time we were watching the band – but, I dunno, it was just a bit funny. It was worth the wait, though. He's a fantastic kisser. I tell you, it's not just his hands he's talented with . . .'

Stella screamed and clapped her hands. 'Yes, yes, yes . . . tell us more!'

'Wait a bit,' gasped Ushi. 'Can you hear yourself, Jodie? You're telling us about him! Intimate details!'

'Yeah,' grinned Jodie. 'Well, I thought it was about time. The two of you have suffered enough.' She was laughing so much, she'd started to shake. 'Oh my God, it's been brilliant watching the two of you trying to worm all the gory details out of me. Best laugh I've had in ages.'

'You mean you've been winding us up?' asked Ushi.

Jodie managed to squeak out a 'Yes'.

'You cow,' Ushi exclaimed, wagging her finger at Jodie. 'But you can just make up for it by telling us everything. The works.'

Jodie was just getting to the exciting bit. Stella and Ushi had barely moved, barely spoken for the past twenty minutes. Glorious countryside was speeding past them but they couldn't have cared less. They were too wrapped up in 'The Max and Jodie Story'.

'So last night, there we were inside his tent after our final supper,' said Jodie. 'Max starts giving me this massage – but practically all-over-body this time instead of the routine stuff . . .'

'What does "practically" mean in this context?' interrupted Ushi. 'Details! We want details!'

'You know,' muttered Jodie, looking embarrassed in case any of the other passengers could hear.

'What do you think "practically" means?' Stella nudged Ushi. 'I'd say it meant pretty much everywhere. Am I right?' she asked Jodie.

Jodie gave a secret little smile. 'Not quite but, yeah, pretty much.'

'Jodie Parker!' Ushi exclaimed. 'Blimey, you're a sly one. What was it like?'

The secret smile grew into a wicked grin.

'Amazing but a bit scary, too. I mean, I've never had that kind of immediate reaction before. It was so strong. I really wanted to . . . I mean, really wanted to, well, . . . Oh, you know . . .'

'And did you?' Ushi and Stella asked at the same time.

Ushi held her breath. She could hardly bear to listen.

Jodie looked at them both for a moment.

'We . . .' she began hesitantly.

'*Excusez-moi mesdemoiselles, vos billets s'il vous plaît!*'

Ushi glared at the railway official who'd just interrupted them. Talk about bad timing!

'Well?' she whispered to Jodie, purposely ignoring him. 'You can't just leave it like this.'

'I bet that's what Max said,' giggled Stella.

'*Vos billets, mesdemoiselles!*' The official was getting a bit stroppy.

Jodie opened her bag, took out her ticket and handed it to him.

'Now's not the right time,' she muttered to Ushi. 'For God's sake show the man your tickets and I'll tell you the rest when he's gone.'

Reluctantly, Stella and Ushi did as she asked. Ushi watched the official with growing impatience. What the hell was he looking so closely at their tickets for? Trust their luck to have landed a 'jobsworth'.

'*Parlez-vous Français?*' he finally asked them.

'*Oui,*' said Jodie. '*Avez-vous un problème?*'

The official immediately launched into quick-fire French of which Ushi couldn't understand a word. She looked at Jodie. She seemed to be having problems, too. She certainly looked confused enough.

'Well?' Stella asked Jodie when the official finally paused for breath.

'It's ridiculous,' said Jodie. 'He says these tickets – our passes – aren't valid for this journey. He says unless we pay the supplement, we've got to get off at the next station.'

'How much is it?' Ushi asked.

'That's the real problem,' said Jodie. 'More than we can afford at the moment. We've hardly any cash, have we? We were going to go to the bank in Toulouse.'

They each scrabbled around in their packs to see

how much they could raise. It came to a grand total of 20F.

'That's nowhere near enough,' moaned Jodie. 'Not even enough to pay for one supplement – let alone three.'

'Can't we just explain our situation?' asked Stella. 'Tell him we'll send the money when we've got it?'

Ushi laughed. 'Oh yeah, he's really going to believe that.'

'Well, I'll try,' said Jodie.

She cleared her throat and started to talk but the official just shook his head.

'It's no good,' she said. 'He's not having any of it. He says we've got to get off. We've no option.'

'Can't we hide in the loos or something?' asked Ushi, getting desperate.

'What, and risk getting into even more trouble?' said Jodie. 'It's not worth it. Besides, –' she glanced up at the official who seemed in no hurry to check the other passengers' tickets. 'I reckon he's hanging around to make sure we do get off.'

The train began to slow down. The next station was obviously approaching.

'But we don't have a clue where we are,' wailed

Stella and started delving around in her pack for her map.

'Somewhere between Bordeaux and Toulouse?' offered Ushi.

'Yeah but where?' said Stella, flicking madly through pages. The train stopped. Ushi peered out of the window and saw nothing but miles and miles of fields. This couldn't be the next proper stop. This place – wherever it was – didn't even have a station. But then she noticed what looked like a tiny platform attached to what looked like an even tinier house.

'*Condom*,' proclaimed a sign on the platform.

They were so hacked off, they couldn't even raise a smile at the name.

'Looks like we're here,' said Ushi. 'Well, *quel* cock-up!'

They ended up sitting on the platform. On their backpacks as the station wasn't large enough to even warrant a bench. It was fryingly hot in the late afternoon sun and there was no shade.

'We've got to get out of here,' said Stella.

'Full marks for observation,' muttered Ushi. 'But just how exactly do we do that? There don't seem to be any taxis or buses. Even if there were, we wouldn't be able to stump up a fare. I've got a credit card but that hardly helps. Who's ever heard of a bus driver saying, 'Oh yes, that'll do nicely!' Oh God, why didn't we go to the bank in Bordeaux before we left?'

'Because we thought we were going to Toulouse,' said Stella. 'And we were going to get cash there.'

'We're going to have to ask someone for help,' said Jodie. 'Maybe there's a campsite near here or a small hotel. We could pay by credit card or maybe cash some travellers cheques there. Well, there's no one around here, is there? I'll go out on a rekkie.'

'Oh no you don't,' said Ushi. 'Look what happened the last time you were let loose on your own! You . . .' She smiled. 'Or did you? That was what you were just about to tell us before we got chucked off that train.'

Jodie shook her head. 'Sorry to disappoint you girls – especially as we find ourselves in such an aptly-named place – but no I didn't. Or rather we didn't. We kissed some more and spent the rest of the time in each others' arms but that was all. It wasn't the right time and we decided we hadn't known each other long enough.'

'I think you did the right thing,' said Stella smiling at Jodie. 'Good for you.'

Ushi nodded but didn't say anymore either. Normally she would have wanted to know loads more – like just how far Jodie had been tempted to go and if she'd made plans to stay in touch with Max. But the moment had passed. Their present predicament had taken precedence over everything else.

'Let's all go on a rekkie,' said Ushi, standing up. 'It's pointless staying here. We're acting like three eccentric old ladies waiting for a non-existent train.'

Half-an-hour later they found themselves in the back of a tractor trailer, chugging down the narrowest road Ushi had ever seen. They'd hailed down the tractor about ten minutes after they'd left the station. They'd never normally be stupid enough to hitch-hike but their luck was in as the driver happened to be a girl around their own age. She told Jodie that there was a campsite a few kilometres away and that they were welcome to a lift.

'Don't know what this place'll be like,' said Jodie, waving goodbye to Lucienne, their chauffeuse, as she deposited them outside the campsite. 'According to Lucienne, most of the clientele are in their forties with a passion for bird watching. Apparently, they get loads of rare breeds in these parts.'

'Fascinating,' said Ushi. 'Not! Who cares, though? It's somewhere to pitch our humble square of canvas.'

'I was rather hoping for a bed for the night,' complained Stella. 'My back's killing me.'

'Ungrateful cow!' exclaimed Ushi. 'You very nearly spent the night on that station. You still might if this campsite doesn't take credit cards.'

'They do!' sighed Jodie in relief as the tractor shuddered to a halt outside reception. 'There's a sign on the door.'

While Ushi sorted out the paperwork for payment, Jodie and Stella went off to start putting up the tent. Ushi gave the reception area a quick once over while her card was being authorised. It was obvious that the clientele were of a more mature nature. There was no blaring music rather softly playing supermarket muzac. And the cards on the noticeboard offered up caravans for sale rather than beat-up combi-vans. Oh well, it was only for a night. There was no way they were going to stay any longer in a place where the three of them were the youngest by about twenty years.

'I retract that,' Ushi said to herself as she caught a quick flash of faded cut offs and a red top – highly un-forty plus wear – flash pass the glass door. She decided to take a closer look. The wearer of the cut-offs and top was ambling across the car park. He turned his head – not for long – but long enough for Ushi to recognise who it was. Jee-zus! Stella was in for a surprise. What the hell was Tomas doing here?

♥

Kiss 'n' Break Up,
Kiss 'n' Make Up!

Week Two
Condom Campsite in South West France

We're in this elephant's graveyard of a campsite in the middle of gawd knows where, when we're supposed to be in 'France's student capital – Toulouse', at least that's what my trusty travel guide reckons to the place. This backwater isn't even in 'old trusty'. The only vaguely exciting thing about it is its name, which suggests a bit of a raunchy past. By the looks of it and the clientele, it sure as hell doesn't have a raunchy present.

At the moment, me and Jodes are having a bit of a sunbathe while Ushi sorts out all the boring paperwork stuff. Hope she remembers to buy a few postcards with 'Greetings from Condom' emblazoned across 'em. Not that I'd dare send one to my folks. Thank heavens for that girl's credit card! If we didn't have it, we'd be right down the Dordogne – or whatever the nearest river to here is called. Tent's up, bags are in! All that girl guide stuff's a cinch now, we've done it so often. Anyway, seeing as though I seem to have a few spare minutes, I decided it was time I gave dear diary a bit of an outing.

I've decided to give up writing in days 'cos I just haven't bothered filling in it – not since St Marion, anyway. So much to see, so much to do and so little time. Blimey, it's scary how time flies – it's no wonder that these clichés catch on. Far as I can work out they're all true!

It's a bit cringy reading back over my last entry written on our last day in St Marion. There I was sitting alone in the campsite caff, swearing undying love for Tomas and all that. Practically willing to sacrifice the rest of the trip for him. Dumb or what? But that's what a touch of the lurve-thang can do for you. And it's me all over to meet someone, decide it's the real thing within hours and then just a few days later, go off 'em. Ushi's right – I go from one extreme to the other. It's like a crush mentality, I guess. A real flash pash. I place lads up on a pedestal then bring the whole contraption *crashing down. Tomas and me had fun but I'm glad now we left St Marion when we did. It was over between us before it could start going wrong. And now he's just a lovely, sexy memory – which is what he should be. Hopefully, I'll have a few more of those before this trip's over.*

Bordeaux was a gas! I'd have hated to have missed it. It got a bit scary when Jodie went AWOL for those few hours of course but, wow, talk about an unexpected outcome. Her revelations on the train were a real eye-opener and dead thrilling. And to think before we left that I wondered – not for long admittedly – whether we might not meet any lads!

I didn't see much bloke action in Bordeaux but I wasn't that bothered. It was good chilling out on my own after all that intensive stuff with Tomas. I don't know what's in store for tonight. Probably zilch in a place like this. I don't mind though. I could do with an uneventful night after Bordeaux.

The Next Morning

Under Canvas

It's spooky! As soon as I get out my diary, things

start to happen. What was I saying about an uneventful night? I must have tempted fate. Last night was like a night of back-to-back soaps. Just thinking about it now makes my head spin.

It started pretty soon after I'd stopped writing. Ushi came back from reception and announced she'd just seen Tomas! I didn't believe her and thought she was taking the mick but she kept saying 'honestly, honestly'. Then I thought she must have seen someone who looked a bit like him. Tomas was a surf dude so what on earth would he be doing here? In bird watchers' paradise?

'Think Stella,' Ushi said. 'Who's he on holiday with?'

'His dad and his uncle,' I said. 'So?'

'And they just happen to be on the crinkly side, right?' she said. 'There something else, too. Didn't I once hear Tomas say that his Onkel Willy liked birds?'

'Yeah, you're right, he did!' said Jodie.

Uh-oh – this was disaster with a capital D for me. I didn't want to know. It made everything slot into place. It made sense that Tomas should be here but I still didn't really believe it.

Then Ushi said that she swore on her own life that it was him and I knew I had to believe her.

Even Ushi wouldn't do things like that as a joke.

'Oh God!' I wailed. 'What am I going to do?' I was so confused. I didn't know whether I wanted to see Tomas again or not. In my mind, I'd ended it. I couldn't see the point in starting the whole thing up again, especially as we were moving on tomorrow. I decided I'd hole up in the tent for the night.

'Don't be daft,' said Jodie. 'What if you go to the loo or something and he sees you? You'd be better facing up to him and telling him how you feel.'

Admirable sentiments perhaps, but I didn't know if I was brave enough for that.

'What do you think?' I asked Ushi.

Ushi shrugged. 'Well you can hide away if you want but I'm not going to – and if Tomas sees me and Jodie then he's automatically going to know you're here too.'

'I could pretend I'm ill,' I said.

'And if he thinks that, what's the first thing he's going to do?' said Ushi. 'Come over all nursey, dash over here with choccies and grapes and the next thing you know he'll be angling to get into your sleeping bag with you!'

'Not if I made out it was something very contagious,' I argued.

Ushi shook her head. 'You're really complicating

*things, Stell. I reckon your best policy is to act
normal and see what happens. No big explanations
or anything like that. Just go with it.'*

So that's what I did.

*I was all nerves walking into the club house a few
hours later. Ushi and Jodie were hungry so we went
first into the restaurant, although I didn't feel like
eating a thing. Thankfully, Tomas wasn't in there
but my eyes never left the door. I kept thinking he'd
walk in at any minute.*

*We went into the bar after that. There was a kind
of disco going on. I was convinced Tomas would
be there, too, but he wasn't. When half-an-hour
went by, I started to relax a bit. Maybe he wasn't
coming at all. Maybe he'd been struck down by
some contagious disease.*

*Some '70s disco started to play and Ushi, embold-
ened by a couple of glasses of the local brew, got up
and started strutting her stuff on the handkerchief-
sized dance floor. Everyone started looking at her
and she really played up to it. As soon as the record
finished, this well-preserved wrinkly rushed over
and asked her to dance. Being Ushi, she said yes.*

*Jodie and I were watching her and laughing
about it when I suddenly saw Tomas walk in with*

his dad – Onkel Willy was no doubt hanging out up a nearby tree studying the habits of the lesser spotted nocturnal sparrow-tit thing. Thankfully, Tomas didn't see me immediately which gave me a bit of time to gather my thoughts and give him a secret once-over. It was strange – he didn't look half so gorge as I remembered. I'd expected his appearance to jump up and sock me between the eyes – like it had on the beach that first time – but there was barely a pat. He looked a bit scruffy – not cool-scruffy but scruffy-scruffy – his hair seemed to have grown and he looked really tired. I looked at his lips but didn't even feel much like snogging him. Weird, eh?

I was tempted to run – in fact, I nearly did – but then he turned and saw me. This incredulous look came over his face and he rushed over to us. He was talking really fast, only stopping to kiss me all over my face. Isn't it odd? One week you can want that more than anything and the next it makes you feel a bit queasy. I pulled away and said a quick hello. He noticed my coolness immediately. That wasn't surprising I guess, the last time I'd seen him I'd been all over him, making a tearful farewell.

Tomas reached for my hand, I pulled away again. Prolonging the agony like this was awful. Maybe

Jodie was right – I should try to tell him how I felt. I decided to go for the jugular.

Entschuldigung, I stammered, hoping I'd got the right German expression for sorry. But I couldn't for the life of me think how to say 'It-was-wonderful-while-it-lasted-but-it-was-just-a-holiday-thing-and-there's-no-point-carrying-on' in his lingo, so I just said, 'Auf Wiedersehen', grabbed Jodie and we ran like the clappers, hoping he wouldn't follow us.

Neither of us expected to find Ushi in the tent. We'd been so wrapped up in the Tomas thing, we hadn't noticed what had been going down on the dance floor. She said she was hiding from the wrinkly she'd been dancing with.

'He came over a bit fruity so I said I was going to the loo and I legged it,' she laughed. 'What did you say to Tomas?'

I quickly told her then decided to change the subject. I wanted Tomas to be history and anyway, I wasn't feeling all that proud of the rather un-brilliant way I'd handled the situation, I hadn't exactly been very nice. Where, I asked the girls, were we heading next? We'd thankfully been able to cash some travellers cheques at the camp office so we were alright for dosh but where to go now?

*That was the question. Although we'd originally
planned to go to Toulouse, I no longer fancied it.
In fact, I was a bit bored with France, period. I
wanted to move on. Luckily the others seemed to
feel the same.*

*'Where to though?' said Ushi. 'Not your aunt
Maria's. Not yet. And I don't feel like beach-
bumming just now either. Know what I really
fancy? I'd love to hit a city – but not just any
old one. I want somewhere that's really buzzy and
happening.'*

*She spread out her map on her sleeping bag and
shone the torch on it. One place jumped out at
us and I was annoyed that I hadn't thought of it
before. Barcelona – it wasn't that far away – just
over the border, in fact. More to the point, as cities
went, you couldn't get much more happening, more
buzzy than that.*

'Barcelona?' I enquired.

'Ólé!' came the reply. 'Viva España!'

Day 13

Barcelona

For the first time I appreciate my Spanish roots!

And I'm not talking onions, either. I felt at ease as soon as we changed trains at the French/Spanish border, and railing into Barcelona, I felt like I'd come home, I love it here! I love the amazing buildings, the rambling streets, the feel of the place. I love the fact that I look like I could easily come from here. And it's great being able to speak the language.

The first day in town, we arrived early evening. We'd already decided we deserved a bit of a treat so we booked ourselves into a small hotel in the centre of town. Right up in the attic we were, but it was fine 'cos the room had three little beds which meant we could share. It was dead dinky actually – like something out of a fairy tale – and the view out of the window was incredible. The three of us stood at that window for ages when we first got there – just looking down at the city sprawled out below, absorbing the atmosphere. It seemed to us like a giant fun fair. I think we were all a bit stunned, too. The sounds of the city after camping out on the coast and in the country sounded outrageously loud to our delicate little lugholes and took some getting used to.

A quick shower and change, and we went out to explore. To be honest, Barcelona seemed a bit dead at first, then I remembered that the Spanish don't go out till really late – 10 or 11 at least. We were about three hours too early but it didn't matter. We walked and walked, taking in the sights. Ushi, fancying herself as a bit of culture-vulture, got totally into it and went off on one of her artsy-farsty rants about the 'fabulously surreal architecture' as she called it.

The shops were something else, too. We gawped in some of the windows of the seriously fashion-able stores, swooned over the designer clothes and completely freaked out when we clocked the prices. Those items that had prices on them, that is. Jodie reckoned if we pooled all the money we'd laid out on this trip, including the price of our tickets, we'd just about be able to afford a dress between us!

The fashions weren't the only thing we gawped at. The Barcelonian lads were something else, too. All black hair, flashing eyes and general all-over-pouty loveliness. But then the Barcelonian girls were pretty hot, as well. They looked so well-groomed and chic. There we were, dolled up in our best togs – Ushi in a pair of fake Versace jeans and little denim jacket, me in a floaty white number and Jodie in a little lycra dress – yet we felt scuzzy and scruffy next to them.

Had something to eat around 10ish – yummy, scrummy tapas – then we hit a couple of bars and ended up in a sweaty, packed-to capacity, neon-lit club. We danced a bit, chatted to a few guys – or at least I did – but I didn't pull. Neither did Jodie. Ushi did of course but then she practically always does. She says she just can't help herself at times and, for her, walking into a club full of tasty-looking lads is the same as walking into a gorgeous-smelling bakery. You always fancy a little something even when you're not particularly hungry! This time she copped off with this Rasta guy with the most amazingly long dreads. He wanted her to go back to his flat. She politely declined! Thank Gawd. Me and Jodes had to kick our heels for a bit while she snogged him goodnight but we eventually got back to the hotel around 3 am, knackered but gagging for more. We'd taken to this town. We decided we wanted to stay.

Day 15

Barcelona

It's unanimous! We love Barcelona which is why we're still here. There's just so much to do in this city, I reckon you could be here forever and still not see it all. We've changed location because we couldn't afford more than one night in a hotel – especially as for most of that night we were out partying. So we're in a youth hostel now and it's fine. It's cheapish, we've hooked up with a good crowd and you don't feel embarrassed if you slurp your coffee at breakfast time like we did at the hotel.

Not that we've seen too many breakfast times. Getting in during the early hours like we do after a night's clubbing, we usually sleep in till 10 or 11. We have a lazy-type brunch at one of the cafés near the hostel, do the culture or shopping bit – OK, the window-shopping bit – in the afternoon then back to the hostel for a quick kip and spruce up for the night ahead. I reckon it's the perfect way to live.

Boy talk? Ushi's seen her Rasta again – once. But he came over all heavy and muttered something about wanting her to have his babies! After that, she told him, less-than-politely, to sling his hook. Since then she's been hanging out with the crowd we've met up with at the youth hostel. She quite fancies this sweetie of a Swedish lad called Bjorn and he seems to like her. They've danced together a few times but no proper lip action, yet. Knowing Ushi, though, that won't be long in coming.

Jodes seems happy enough just to chill out to the music and have a laugh at the moment. I think the Max Factor's still big with her and she's not interested in anyone else right now. As for moi – or should I say moy? Well, I've had a few dances and the occasional snog with Italian Guido, another lad from our hostel but that's all. He's nice, but not that nice.

Day 17

Barcelona

Sadly our last day in this top, top city. Just time to squeeze in a final bout of sight-seeing and then we're off. A regretful decision we came to over breakfast (we made it for once!) as the three of us worked out just how much money we had left. Basically, we're going through the dosh in this town like there's no tomorrow and we just can't afford to stay here any longer. It's tempting to run up a bill on Ushi's credit card. Ushi says she doesn't mind and neither would her mum, but the thing is, money's not the only commodity we're running short of. It's scary how quickly the time's passing too. We've been gone over two weeks already yet it seems like only a matter of hours ago since we were on that ferry heaving our guts up. We've still got to go to Aunt Maria's and then we all fancy a chill-out spell on a beach to soak up a final ray blast before we take the express train back up through France to Boulogne. Lloret de Mar on the Costa Brava sounds like it was put there with us in mind. The guide book describes it as being a haven for those who like their nightlife 'loud, late and libidinous'. After an oh-so-quiet spell at Auntie's mountain home, I just know we'll be gagging for all of that! So y'see, we gotta go now 'else we won't fit it all in. It feels like we've done miles and miles but looking at the map of Europe makes you realise just how much more there is to see.

'Next year . . .' says Jodie.

Yes please! I feel like booking my ticket now!

After brekkie, I go and phone Auntie – thinking about it, I'm amazed she's on the phone – to tell her to expect us in the evening. She's almost beside herself with excitement at the prospect of our visit. I guess in the backwater she lives in, it's like she's expecting the second coming!

'And such luck,' she babbles just before I put down the phone. 'Your timing could not be better.'

'Why?' I ask, momentarily excited myself. What's going down up there? A festival perhaps? Like the one in Bordeaux?

I cross my fingers, but by the time Aunt Maria's told me what it's all about, I feel like shoving them down my throat.

'Your cousin, Miguel, is due home from university,' she chuckles. 'He comes tomorrow and will be so pleased to see you.'

I ring off feeling completely devoid of excitement and anticipation at that prospect. She calls that lucky? Well, that kind of luck I reckon we can do without.

♥

Love 'n' War

'Miles from anywhere,' Stella had said on the ferry crossing. 'In the middle of nowhere . . .' Arriving in the Valle d'Aran, the area of the Pyrenees where Aunt Maria's village was situated, Jodie could see what Stella had meant. It sure was remote. The train, the smallest one they'd travelled on so far, seemed to have taken ages from Barcelona and had literally chugged its way up mountains, down valleys and back up the otherside again. But there was no doubting that it was pretty. With the majestic Pyrenean mountains as a backdrop, it was, Jodie thought, one of the most picturesque places she'd been to. And the air was so fresh, she wanted to drink it.

Aunt Maria's three-storey house had a definite Alpine feel to it. Once again, she, Stella and Ushi were sharing an attic room – like they'd done that first night in Barcelona. But the view from this window couldn't have been more different. Taking in the mountain air and marvelling at how green the valleys were the morning after they'd arrived, Jodie had felt a bit like Heidi – the heroine of her favourite childhood story.

Mmmmm, mmmm, Jodie reflected, it would no doubt be numb-skullingly boring to stay here for any length of time. But four or five days sleeping in a comfy, cosy bed, eating home-cooked food and being thoroughly spoilt wasn't to be sniffed at. While she'd hardly have come here out of choice, now she was here it made sense to make the best of it. She was sure they'd be able to find something to do. Like, er, swimming, for instance. They could go for a dip – or ten – in one of the lakes nearby.

Yeah, thinking about it, some kind of energetic, sporting activity would be a good idea. Exhaust their minds and bodies so they'd be too knackered to imagine what might have been going down in this oh-so-romantic setting if only the right lads were around. She kept seeing herself and Max walking arm-in-arm through the countryside and lying down together in the lush, green meadows. The sweet smell of newly cut grass and the even sweeter smell of Max's skin, the feel of his lips on hers and those magic hands of his massaging her into a state of pure bliss. Ooooooooh, if only he were here now, she'd . . . But then in another way, Jodie was glad he wasn't. They'd had a fab couple of days in Bordeaux but it had been a one off – they'd both known that. She'd never forget Max but, hey let's get real, holiday romances didn't travel well. Look at Stella and Tomas, for instance. When they'd met up again, it had been a disaster and now – and in the future – when Stella thought about Tomas, she'd remember their unhappy last meeting in Condom rather than all the lovely, luv'd-up stuff in St Marion.

After lunch, Jodie and Ushi had offered to go down to the nearest village and do some shopping for Aunt Maria's special celebration supper which she'd planned to welcome both them and the returning Miguel to the mountain homestead. Jodie and Ushi's offer hadn't been made entirely unselfishly. Following a morning of Spanish family gossip, they'd both wanted to get out of the house while Stella and her auntie caught up on more news.

'What are you thinking about?' Ushi went on as they walked down the steep pathway leading to the village. 'Wondering just what we're going to do with ourselves in this mountain retreat?'

'Kind-of,' mumured Jodie. 'And thinking about life, love and the universe.'

'Oh Gawd, don't go all philosophical on me,' muttered Ushi. 'You know, you haven't been the same since you had that massage in Bordeaux!'

'You're right there,' sighed Jodie dreamily.

They turned a corner, and a few shops and some village folk came into view.

'At last! Provisions!' exclaimed Ushi. 'Hey up, Jodes, have we come out with our knickers at half-mast or something? Have we got porridge all over our faces? Because we seem to be attracting quite a few stares.'

'Hardly surprising, is it?' Jodie commented. 'I mean we're strangers in these here parts.'

Ushi giggled as two young girls of around ten stared at her in amazement and obvious admiration.

'Y'know, I quite like it. Must be what being a celeb feels like.'

'Well, cast your mind back to ... what is it?' Jodie peered at Aunt Maria's shopping list. '*Cebollas* rather than celebs. That's onions to you!' She opened the door to the first shop they came across – a kind of deli-cum-greengrocers. 'Now this should be fun – neither of us speaks a word of Spanish nor the local dialect, either. Aunt Maria must be bonkers trusting us to do her shopping for her. I reckon we should hand the shopkeeper the list. And hand over the money. Yeh?'

'Absolutely!' Ushi agreed.

The shopkeeper was just wrapping up their purchases when Jodie spotted what looked like a large loaf of bread entirely covered in sugar. On impulse, she gestured to the owner that she wanted to buy a loaf.

'Eh?' piped-up Ushi. 'Is that on Auntie's list?'

Jodie shook her head. 'I want to contribute to supper, though. I think we should – as a kind of thanks to Aunt Maria for having us.'

'Nice idea, Jodes,' said Ushi as they left the shop. 'It is sweet of her to put all three of us up. But I just wish . . .' She paused suddenly. 'Ohmigod!' Her voice had become a squeak. 'Ohmigod – take at look at that! Ohmigod! Forget what I just said. Suddenly I love it here. I think I must be in heaven!'

Jodie looked at what, or rather who, Ushi was staring at and immediately felt herself being unfaithful to the memory of Max. Sitting across the street, sipping coffee at a dinky pavement café, was, quite simply, one of the best-looking lads Jodie reckoned she'd ever seen. Movie stars, pop stars, world famous sports stars . . . they had nothing on this bloke. He was utterly, utterly droolsome! Black, black hair which flopped silkily across his forehead, flawless olivey skin, perfectly chiselled nose and a full, sensuous mouth – he was a veritible portrait of gorgeousness.

Sensing he was being gawped at, he looked up suddenly and Jodie felt like her heart was in her mouth – or the other way round. His eyes – languid and golden hazelly-green – stared straight into hers. Jodie couldn't tear her eyes away. It was as if they'd been artificially fixed in one position and were unable to move. Finally, he smiled at her, raised his coffee cup to her, got up from the table and walked away. Jodie shuddered with excitement – he fancied her! She knew he did. That look he'd just given her had been a definite I-want-to-snog-the-lips-off-you kind of look. And my God was it mutual! She watched him walk down the street. He had to be at least six foot and he swaggered slightly – like a sexy cowboy.

'Ooooooh!' murmured Ushi in her ear. 'Oooooh, oooooh, oooooh! Did you see him? More importantly, did you see the way he was eyeing me up?

♥ 115 ♥

That lad's got the hots for me and he's left me all of a sizzle! Ahhhhh! I'm not going to let him get away. Let's follow him.'

Jodie was too shocked to reply. Ushi thought he'd been staring at her? Well, she was wrong about that. One hundred and ten per cent wrong. He'd been looking at *her* not Ushi. She just knew it! Could feel it deep, deep down inside.

'But . . .' Jodie started to say, then she changed her mind. If Ushi was convinced that this lad fancied her, there's no way she'd just say, 'Yes, OK, Jodes – you're right' when Jodie informed her that she'd merely been thinking wishfully. It was far more likely, she'd storm up the street after him, stop him and demand to know exactly for whose benefit the flirty eye action had been for. And that, for embarrassment and cringe-making value, just didn't bear thinking about. Much better to play dumb – for now.

'We can't follow him, Ush,' said Jodie. 'We've still got stuff to buy and Auntie's expecting us back. We'll have to let him go.'

Making whimpering noises like an injured puppy, Ushi followed Jodie into the butcher's. Once again, Jodie handed over a list but they could have given her back pig swill ingredients for all she cared.

She kept seeing golden-green eyes looking at her. At *her*, she was positive they'd been looking at her. Inwardly, she started to panic. Oh God, she might never see him again. She should have tried to make some excuse to Ushi and gone after him. But suddenly she felt calm again. They were here for the best part of a week, weren't they? In a tiny place like this, she was bound to run into him again. In fact, Jodie decided with a sudden burst of determination, she was going to do everything in her power to make sure of it.

Dear Davy - why haven't you written? I arrived at Stella's aunty's expecting to find a lovely, long letter from you. I wrote the address on that postcard I sent you from contraceptive campsite in France so you've no excuse, my lad!! Spain's great - Barcelona especially. After we've taken the mountain air, we're off to Lloret for a bit more sun-soaking and cool camping...

Ushi threw down her pen. She couldn't be bothered to write to Davy at the moment. Couldn't give him her full attention. But then that seemed to be true of everything. It was early evening now but since spotting that gorgeous guy at the shops, she'd spent practically the whole afternoon thinking about him. There'd been something dead fascinating about him. So many unanswered questions about him, too. Questions she was desperate to know the answers to. Like what, for instance, was somebody who looked like him doing in a place like this?

'You'd better get changed, Ushi,' said Stella who'd just walked into their room, fresh from the shower. 'You too, Jodie.'

'What for?' Ushi muttered. 'We're not going anywhere, are we?'

'No but my auntie's been slaving over a hot stove all afternoon.' Stella started drying her hair. 'She doesn't get that many visitors so our being here is a big thing for her. And she wants it to be special.'

'I know, I know,' sighed Ushi and slowly got up from her bed. 'I was thinking, Stell . . .' she said, her voice momentarily muffled as she riffled through her rucksack looking for something to wear. 'After supper, d'you think your aunt would mind if we, er, schlepped down to the village for a bit?'

'What for?' Stella asked. 'There's nothing to do and nowhere to go apart from sitting sipping coffees with the locals and watching a very tiny corner of the world go by.' She grinned suddenly. 'Oh I get it! You want to go down to the village to see if this apparently gorgeous lad's there, yeah?'

Ushi looked at her sheepishly.

'Might do,' she said.

Stella shook her head. 'I've already told you, Ush. He must have been a figment of your imagination. There aren't any lads like the one you described living up here. You must be suffering from altitude sickness and be hallucinating with it. Either that – or he's a wind-up. You and Jodes having me on about some amazing bloke who doesn't even exist.'

'Oh he exists alright, doesn't he, Jodie?' said Ushi.

Jodie nodded. 'He sure does but, er, you're right about one thing Stella . . .' It was time, Jodie suddenly decided, that Ushi faced up to reality – that it had been *her* he'd eyed up, not Ushi – if only because Ushi had been going on

♥ 119 ♥

about him all afternoon like he was her private property, and Jodie was sick of it. 'I reckon Ush's imagination must be playing a few tricks on her 'cos, er, sorry Ush . . . I don't exactly know how to put this so I may as well come straight out with it . . . I'm pretty sure he was looking at me, eyeing me up rather than you. In fact, I'm positive.'

'What?' Ushi exclaimed, puzzled. 'You don't think . . . ?' She shook her head. 'Oh Jodes, I'm sorry but . . . I mean you were standing next to me so I can understand the mistake but no, really, he was eyeing me up. I'm absolutely sure of that.'

'Yeah, well I'm just as sure it was me,' said Jodie, resolutely.

'I saw him first,' Ushi came back with. 'You'd never have noticed him if I hadn't pointed him out.'

'So?' Jodie shrugged. 'What's that got to do with anything? You . . .'

'Girls, girls, girls . . .' interrupted Stella. 'I can't believe I'm hearing this. Fighting over a lad, for God's sake! A lad, by the way, whom I still don't really believes exists. I know what you two are like, especially if you're a bit bored. Wind-up merchants, the pair of you. This little scenario might all be for my benefit. But if it's not, well . . . you should just hear yourselves! I thought we'd agreed eons ago that no bloke's worth arguing about – however gorge he might be.'

'You didn't see him,' muttered Jodie. 'Anyway, that's not the point.'

'What is the point?' asked Ushi.

'That you've got the wrong end of the stick, Ush. I don't want to fall out about this but you have. It was . . .'

'Oh not again!' Stella yelled. 'Enough! Can't we just leave it for now? Maybe he was eyeing up the pair of you.'

'No way,' Jodie hit back with.

'That we do agree on,' said Ushi.

'I'll tell you what,' suggested Stella. 'OK, we will go into the village after supper. If he's there, I'll act as ref and decide which of the two of you he fancies.' She started to laugh. ''Course we might be able to solve it a whole lot easier than that. He might just fancy me!' Ushi joined in the laughter but she felt deadly serious inside. She'd never felt so determined. He was hers and if any of them was going to pull him, she was.

Just then Aunt Maria called up the stairs.

'What did she say?' asked Jodie.

Stella sighed. 'Oh to hurry up and come down because Miguel's just arrived. My oh-so-dreary cousin. That's all we need.'

Ushi quickly slipped off her wrap and pulled on her fake Versaces and a silk shirt. She'd forgotten all about Stella's cousin, too wrapped up in her thoughts and fantasies about 'lurve-stuff-on-legs', as she'd named him. She sincerely hoped that Miguel was a fast eater who had very little to say. 'Cos the sooner this supper was over, the sooner she could run down to the village and the sooner she might see L.S.O.L.

*

'So where is he then?' asked Ushi as the three of them sat down at the dining-room table. 'The "magnetic" Miguel. Not!'

'Just getting changed, apparently,' replied Stella. 'He'll be down in a minute. God, I hope he's improved since the last time I saw him. We didn't exactly part on good terms. I put melted choccie in his Action Man's trousers which seemed to upset him no end and . . .'

'So I hang up your Barbie by her hair,' a lightly-accented voice called down the stairs. Miguel, obviously. Well, thought Ushi just before she turned round to take a look at him, his voice sure didn't sound wussy. It was a little bit sexy actually. It would be interesting to see what the rest of him was like.

She was sitting with her back to the doorway and didn't see him walk in. But what she did see was a look of total amazment of Stella's face while Jodie's expression . . . well, there was no other word for it, was totally rapt.

Ushi slowly turned her head and found herself gazing into a pair of sleepy-green eyes. She'd been here before. It was him – Mr Gorgeous was standing right here in Auntie Maria's dining-room! She didn't understand. This dish was 'manky' Miguel? Stella's dweeb of a cousin? It didn't make sense.

'You've changed,' Ushi heard Stella say, in a kind of cross between a gulp and a gasp.

'You too,' murmured Miguel. 'You're . . . you're really pretty, *chicita!*'

He kissed her soundly on both cheeks which by now were glowing. Stella had come over all preeny. So she fancied him, too. That much was already clear from the ga-ga look on her face, the sound of her voice and the way she'd suddenly kicked into major, hair-flinging flirtation mode.

Were cousins allowed to fancy each other? Ushi didn't know.

'Introduce us!' Ushi hissed.

'Oh yes,' gushed Stella. 'Jodie and Ushi, this is my cousin, er, Miguel.'

'*Hola*,' Miguel smiled first at Ushi and then Jodie.

Ushi was just about to mention their kind-of meeting earlier when Aunt Maria bustled in, carrying a steaming pot of delicious-smelling food and beaming all over her face. She said something and then burst out laughing.

'What did she say?' Ushi asked Stella but Miguel answered for her.

'That never before has she prepared such a welcome for me,' he said, smiling at Ushi and revealing a set of perfect white teeth. 'I have to say, yes, that is true.'

Oh wow! thought Ushi. He is just so gorgeous! She suddenly felt all light-headed. This was too good to be true. All afternoon, she'd been brooding on how she might find him again and now here he was – sleeping under the very same roof! She hadn't particularly been looking forward to this part of the trip but now, against all the odds, it had the potential to turn into the best bit!

Ushi spent the rest of the meal in a bit of a daze. The food was delicious but she'd hardly tasted a thing. She was too busy at first watching Miguel and then too busy trying to make him laugh – not exactly easy when she was having to compete with full-on flirt attacks from Stella and Jodie. One point in her favour was that, to her delight, she'd discovered that Miguel was studying art and design at college like she was. But whenever she'd try and engage him in some relevant conversation, Stella would produce another 'Action Man' type reminiscence from up her sleeve.

Then Jodie leapt up, disappeared into the kitchen and returned bearing the sugar loaf.

'I bought it as a surprise,' she said, suddenly blushing up. 'To say thanks to Aunt Maria for having us.'

'That is so sweet of you,' murmured Miguel and briefly stroked Jodie's hand which made her blush even more.

'*Er, excuse me!*' Ushi had wanted to yell across the table. '*I was there when she bought it. I thought it was a sweet idea, too. So don't I deserve a hand-stroke, too?*'

'It's sugar loaf,' Jodie said smiling at Miguel. 'No, no,' he responded. 'This is *Sal Pan* – salt bread – not *Azucar Pan*. You're so funny . . .' He started to laugh. 'It's lucky you didn't put some honey on it to eat too . . . Very delicious,' he was really laughing now.

'I . . . I . . . I . . .' Jodie started to stammer.

Quite unexpectedly, Stella started to giggle too. She licked her finger, tentatively touched her piece of bread, then licked her finger again. She grimaced. 'Good choice, Jodes!'

Ushi started to laugh too. She expected Jodie to start tittering too but she didn't. Her emotions were obviously running high because she started to blub.

Aunt Maria immediately started fussing round her while Miguel did even more. This time, in addition to Jodie's hand, her stroked her hair and put his arm round her! Aghhhhhhhh!

'*Er, excuse me*,' Ushi wanted to yell again. '*I was there when she bought it. It was my fault too. So don't I deserve a bit of a hug, as well?*'

After supper Stella, Ushi and Jodie cleared away the dishes, leaving Aunt Maria and Miguel to have a bit of a chinwag.

'You'll be glad to know that Auntie's cool about us going down the village, Ush,' said Stella. 'She wants to spend some time alone with Miguel. She's a bit narked because he didn't come straight home when he arrived. He went to an old school-friend's instead.'

Ushi grinned. 'Oh I, er, don't think I want to go to the village any more . . . Come on Stella! As if I need to tell you why! He's here – the gorgeous creature I was telling you about. He's only your cousin! The cousin you've been slagging ever since we came away. Blimey, if I'd known he what he was really like . . .'

'How was I to know? His metamorphosis has come as a real shock to me, too,' Stella admitted. 'Auntie neglected to tell me just how gorgeous he'd got – although she did mention he'd changed a bit.'

'He's simply beautiful,' Jodie piped up suddenly.

'Isn't he?' beamed Stella, sounding very territorial. 'Totally droolsome.'

'He's just stunning,' breathed Ushi.

She looked at the other two. They looked at her. And she knew they were all thinking the same thing. This was weird! In all the years they'd been mates, they'd never gone after, or really been attracted to, the same lad. Whenever it had got close to happening before, one or two of them would always back down without argument. Or they'd all decide that none of them fancied him, anyway. But this time, Ushi sensed, was different. There was a definite whiff of war in the air. They all fancied the cute little bum off him and not one of them was going to give in without a fight. Maybe they should go down to the village after all. They had things to discuss. Miguel.

Day 19

Aunt Maria's
I'm dog-tired but I'm making myself write this because I feel tonight has been a night of momentous importance. First up, I discover that my cousin's no longer a weedy little caterpillar but a fabulous, totally amazing butterfly. Second-up, within about a nanosecond of seeing him again after all these years I realise I fancy him like crazy and third up, it takes me about another nanosecond to clock that Ush and Jodie are feeling exactly the same as me. Our little post-supper chat definitely confirmed this. We all fancy Miguel, we all want him and not one of us is willing to back down. It would be a damned sight easier if (a) he had

a steady girlfriend but one bit of family gossip I absorbed today was that there's no one special in his life. When Aunt Maria told me this, I presumed it was because he couldn't get anyone to go out with him but now I realise the reverse is true. He must have so many girlies gagging for him, he must have a ball playing the field. And (b)? Well, it would also make things easier for us three gals if Mig made it clear just who he likes best. I'm usually pretty hot at picking up pheromones but tonight, I wasn't. I can see why Ush and Jodes were arguing about which of them he'd been looking at when they saw him in the village because he's got this way with him. He's a complete charmer who probably gives every girl he meets the impression that he's really into them.

Anyway after supper, Ush, Jodes and me go down to the village for a coffee. It's like any other night since we've been away except it's not. We're laughing and joking with each other as usual, but tonight there's a definite undercurrent of tension as well. It's about Miguel. We're just getting stuck in to our cappucinos when I decide I can't stand it any longer. Something has to be said.

'We all fancy him, right?' I blurt out.

We're actually in the middle of talking about something else but Ush and Jodie are onto the wave-length immediately.

'Yep,' *says Ush while Jodie just nods.*

There's silence. Stalemate. Each of us waiting for the other to say 'OK – forget it. Forget him. Count me out.' *It doesn't happen.* 'Then we've no choice,' *I say eventually.* 'It has to be a three-girl contest.'

'But you're his cousin,' *Jodie says.*

'So?' *I shrug.* 'That's got nothing to do with it. It's not illegal to marry your cousin, let alone snog 'em. Anyway, it's not the matrimony bit I'm interested in.'

'Yeah, yeah, alright . . .' *says Jodie.*

'Open combat then,' *muses Ushi.* 'Is this wise?' *A competitive gleam comes into her eye.* 'Yes, why not? If nothing else it'll give us something interesting to do while we're here. A new project to wile away the time. It'll be a laugh. But I'm warning you both, you don't stand a chance.'

Jodie and I smirk at this. 'Ush,' *I say.* 'You're just too modest!'

'You may mock,' *says Ushi.* 'But I mean it.'

'Yeah, well,' *says Jodie, lowering her voice, licking her lips and running her fingers through* her hair. 'You've never really been in competition with me before, have you, darling?'

'Me neither,' I say.

'You two don't worry me, darlings!' Ushi comes back with.

We're all laughing but underneath it all, we're serious. We've never had this kind of conversation before, never been love rivals before – not properly anyway – and I'm not sure that I like it.

'A nice, clean fight then?' says Jodie. 'We're all agreed? We all go for it – or rather him? And no hard feelings?'

'Absolutely,' says Ushi. 'I think we're mature enough to handle it – or rather him – whatever the outcome!'

For a moment, I feel panicky. But it passes. Yeah, it'll be fine. Like Ushi says, we're sensible enough to cope with it. And we're best mates. The best ever. Nothing can alter that. I raise my coffee cup. 'To us!' I announce. 'And to Miguel, God help him and may the best girl win!'

♥

Babes In Battle!

Instead of a free-for-all where the three of them would constantly be vying for Miguel's attention, they decided – before going down for breakfast the next morning – on a structured game, or rather pulling, plan.

'A kind of Miguel mesh,' giggled Ushi.

'I guess,' said Stella.

'There's a "do" down in the village the night after next,' said Jodie. 'We saw that poster in the café, remember? Well, I reckon we should aim to have the sitch sorted by then. Yeah?' Both Stella and Ushi nodded.

'So how do we divide the time up before then?' asked Stella. 'God, it's complicated isn't it? Not to mention calculated!'

'Well sometimes you have to be,' Jodie went on briskly. 'This is a competition and you have to be organised in competitions else they don't work.

Alright then, who's going first?'

'Eh?' asked Ushi.

'. . . And I suppose we should discuss exactly what we each intend to do with him,' Jodie continued.

'Isn't that a bit personal?' giggled Stella.

Jodie shook her head. 'Not like that. I'm talking about specific plans of attack.'

'Oh I get it,' said Ushi suddenly. 'Like, Miguel and me obviously have art 'n stuff in common so I ask him to show me round the nearest gallery or something?'

'Right!' smiled Jodie. 'And I love swimming so I'll ask him to come for a dip with me in the nearest lake.'

'Oh great!' Stella pouted. 'Ush gets to be all artsy and romantic with him, you get to swim with him – which means you'll get to see each other nearly naked – and I get to . . . what? Reminisce about Action Man, "Kerplunk" and the Spanish version of "Mousetrap" some more?'

'Well you seemed more than happy with that last night,' muttered Ushi. 'On and on and on, you went.'

'Yeah, well, I reckon I've pretty much mined that vein now,' said Stella. 'And besides, that kind of thing's hardly going to get him in a smoochy-moochy frame of mind, is it? I want him to see me as I am now, not as some brat of a kid who constantly fought with him.'

'Stell . . .' Ushi wagged a finger at her. 'He only has to look at you to see that. What did he call you last night? A *chicita*? I don't know what it means but it sounds dead nice.'

'Plus you have a joint history,' said Jodie. '*And* you speak his language. There'll be no awkward silences for you, will there?'

'I guess not,' said Stella, looking marginally happier. 'What else then, Jodes? What's next? You seem to have this whole crazy thing worked out.'

'We work out who goes when,' said Jodie. 'For instance – me this afternoon, Ush tomorrow and you, Stell, the next day. I reckon we've got to space it a bit – poor lad will be confused if we don't allow him a rest between each of us. Basically, we each go out and give it our best shot.'

'And rules . . .' mused Ushi. 'We must have rules.'

'Like what?' asked Jodie, surprised.

'Like we don't give each other any kind of bad press,' said Ushi. 'You know . . . like mentioning other squeezes – holiday or otherwise – in order to score extra points ourselves.'

'Oh come on!' replied Jodie. 'As if.'

'Ush, honestly . . .' tutted Stella.

'We might,' said Ushi. 'You never know, we just might. I'm only being realistic. I can get pretty competitive when I'm roused – we all can. We all like winning, don't we? And if the going gets tough, I bet we'll be tempted to, too. So we're fair about each other. Like if Mig says something like, 'I'm really into you but what about your friends?' we come back with something like, 'Oh that's fine. Don't worry. We're all pretty cool about this sort of thing'. She paused to take a breath. 'And another thing – we don't butt in on each other's time, we stay out of the way, plus . . . we keep schtum on what occurs on each of our dates. We don't want to put each other off. That, I think, will be the hardest thing of all . . .'

'And . . .' Stella added finally. 'We don't wind each other up. However tempting it might be.'

'Absolutely,' said Ushi and Jodie together.

Suddenly they heard the man himself calling to his mum. He was already downstairs. 'Go on then, Jodes!' Ushi gave her a nudge. 'There's no time like the present. Off you jolly well go!'

*

Splash!

Perched on a rock like the little mermaid, Jodie admired the spectacle of a tanned, tautly-lean Miguel diving into the mirror-like surface of the lake. In spite of the confident exterior she'd shown to Ush and Stella, and in spite of the fact she was truly confident that he fancied her, she'd been pretty damned nervous about asking Mig out.

'I was wondering . . .' she'd said to him. 'Is there anywhere to go for a swim round here? It's such a gorgeous day.'

'Sure,' he'd replied with a lazy smile. 'There is *La Panta de la Torcassa*. There is wonderful swimming there.'

'Where is it, exactly?' she'd said, although having read up on the area she already had a pretty good idea.

He'd started to explain but then he'd said, just as she'd hoped he would, 'I think it would be easier if I showed you. You'd mind . . . if I came along? Stella and Ushi . . .'

'Oh it's just me,' she'd come back with. 'The others are, er, busy. OK?'

Miguel smiled again and said, 'Fine, no problem' and if he had any notions that the whole thing might be a set-up, he sure wasn't letting on.

Jodie glanced at her watch. She was trying terribly hard not to be but she couldn't help feeling just the weeniest bit impatient. They'd been here for almost two hours. They'd shared a picnic in a deserted spot, chatted at length about their respective colleges and courses, read a little, swam a little and sunbathed a little. But in spite of all this, and the not inconsiderable fact that she happened to be wearing her grooviest swimsuit, which made her stomach look really flat and her legs look almost as long as Ushi's, if she was honest with herself, she didn't feel she'd made much progress. Certainly nowhere as much as she'd hoped. It wasn't that Miguel was being 'off' with her, he just wasn't being especially 'on'. True, he smiled a lot and seemed quite interested in what she had to say but, well, nothing else. Nothing very intimate. It was as if he was holding back. Maybe she'd imagined that he'd been eyeing her up in the first place. Maybe – and this was the rub – he really did fancy Ush – or even cousin Stella. Well that had to be nipped in the bud, pronto.

Now battle had commenced, she wanted, but really, wanted to win. In many ways, the 'prize' had become immaterial.

Watching Miguel climb out of the water, Jodie

got up and quickly walked back to the grassy area of shore where they'd been previously. It was now or never. When he came and laid back down next to her, she'd take some seriously decisive action.

'Good swim?' she asked as he sat down.

He nodded, his teeth chattering loudly. Jodie lightly touched his arm. 'OOOOOh, you're freezing. Here . . . borrow my towel.' She made to put her towel round his shoulders and suddenly found her face just centimetres away from his. Jodie moved closer until her lips brushed his. She started to kiss him, expecting his mouth to be as eager as hers but he seemed completely frozen, and she couldn't help feeling disappointed.

'I think we should go soon,' mumbled Miguel hurridly as soon as Jodie had pulled away. 'It will be late by the time we get back.' Jodie decided to go for the jugular. Despite the embarrassment of the failed kiss, the way she saw it, she didn't have much to lose.

'The village bash on Thursday . . .' she began. 'What d'you think it will be like?'

Miguel grinned. 'Much as you would expect. Why? Will you be going?'

Jodie felt suddenly encouraged. Maybe it was just that Miguel wanted to take things slowly. Not exactly a prime consideration of hers at the moment with the ever-present spectre of a predatory Ushi and Stella hovering at the back of her mind. This was her one chance at trying to get Miguel in her camp and she wasn't doing too brilliantly thus far.

'Yeah, probably,' she grinned back. 'How about you?'

'Maybe . . . Will Stella and Ushi want to go also, do you think?'

Rats! Now why had he suddenly brought them up? Just when relations between them – despite the mediocre snog – had seemed on the up again. There was only one possible reason. Because he fancied them, that's why.

'Oh I doubt it,' Jodie heard herself saying. 'It's not really their scene. They'll probably prefer to spend the night writing to their boyfriends. Ushi's got this heavy thing with a lad at home while Stella met Tomas in France and she's mad about him.'

Ohmigod, she'd gone and done it! Brought up the other lads in Ushi's and Stella's lives. She'd snitched, she'd fibbed, she'd blabbed. She hadn't meant to – honest she hadn't. It had just slipped out – like a reflex action, a defence mechanism. She felt terrible but not that terrible as she saw Miguel nodding with obvious understanding at what she'd just said.

'I see,' he murmured. 'Well, certainly I will be going. It wouldn't do for you to be alone. Apart from Aunt Maria, you do not know anyone here.'

Yes!!!!!! Yes!!!!!! Yes!!!!!! Jodie just restrained herself from punching the air. She'd done it. She was sure she had. It, or rather he, was in the bag!

'Well?' Ushi and Stella demanded to know once they'd gone to bed that night – the first chance they'd had to talk properly since Jodie and Miguel had returned. 'How did it go?'

Jodie allowed herself a superior little smile although deep down, now, she didn't feel quite so confident. Over supper, Miguel hadn't paid her any special attention. He'd been just as into Stella and Ushi, and had seemed positively keen when Ush had suggested making a trip to the nearest art gallery. Still, maybe she was reading too much into it. He *had* snogged her and even more importantly, he'd more-or-less promised to hang out with her at the festival.

'Fine,' Jodie had smiled mysteriously. 'But of course, I'm not at liberty to tell you any more. We agreed, didn't we?'

'Awwwww,' groaned Ushi. 'Just a few of the

juiciest bits! Go on – like did you pull?' Jodie shook her head and tapped her nose. 'That's for me to know and you to find out!'

Ushi couldn't quite work out where she was going wrong. On the surface, it was all going swimmingly. Showing her around the gallery, Miguel was being as charming as ever – pointing out specific paintings he thought she'd be interested in, laughing with her at the patently awful ones, taking time to give her the lowdown on local painters ... It was all undoubtedly interesting but not exactly what she wanted to hear. She'd been hoping for something more on the lines of '*You're gorgeous Ushi! How can I concentrate on still-life when the real life I'm presently experiencing is far more appealing ...*' At which point, Miguel would insist on leading her out of the gallery to some quiet, private place where they could be alone and get to experience a little more than each other's opinions on brush techniques.

There was, Ushi decided, a definite – albeit invisible – barrier between Miguel and herself. A barrier she was pretty sure would answer to the name of Jodie. Despite the fact that Miguel hadn't seemed particularly into Jodes over supper last night, that had evidently been a ploy. No doubt dreamt up by Jodie to make it seem all the more interesting. On the other hand, though, he didn't react in the slightest whenever she mentioned Jodie. What she needed was some definite way of knowing exactly how she felt about her. Stella she wasn't too worried about. She was his cousin, for God's sake! And although they hadn't seen each other for years, Ushi felt sure that their old brother–sister type relationship would make it impossible for them to suddenly form a new romantic type one. No, Jodie was definitely the one to be watched.

'Did, er, Jodie tell you anything about the music festival we went to in France?' Ushi began, innocently enough.

Miguel shook his head. Aha! thought Ushi.

'We had the best time,' Ushi went on. 'Jodie especially.'

'Why Jodie?' asked Miguel.

'Oh she hooked up with a celeb's brother,' said Ushi. 'Got backstage passes – the lot. Oh yes, Max *was* gorgeous – no doubt about that. I still think she's really into him.'

Oooops! She hadn't meant to mention Max – at least, not consciously. He'd just kind of slipped out kind of naturally. She couldn't have mentioned

Bordeaux and not mentioned Max. Ushi felt guilty but then decided such an emotion was pointless. To hell with it! This was each girl for herself.

Now was it her imagination or was Miguel now looking at her in a different light. He seemed to be looking *at* her for a start, rather than beyond her.

'No music festivals happening around here, then?' Ushi said, hoping this particular line of questioning might lead somewhere.

Miguel smiled and shook his head.

'Just the same village party that happens every year,' he said. 'You think you will go?'

'I think I might,' Ushi said. 'And you?'

Miguel shrugged. 'Of course – as always.'

Ushi smiled. Mig smiled back. It didn't tell her everything she wanted to know but it would do. For now.

That evening there were opportunities aplenty to discuss tactics as Miguel took Aunt Maria out to visit a friend. Ushi, however, despite pleadings from Stella and Jodie was keeping schtum, as agreed.

'You next, Stell,' said Jodie. 'Any ideas? You must have. You've been going on about it all day.'

Stella shook her head. 'I've decided it's best to keep it simple,' she said. 'I'm not making any plans. I'll see what occurs tomorrow and take it from there.'

'Oooo, you little risk-taker, you,' said Ushi. 'Playing the spontaneity card, eh?'

'I think it's best,' said Stella.

The next morning, however, she'd changed her mind. She'd got up and gone downstairs early in order to nab Miguel. She had it all worked out. It would be simple but effective. They'd walk into the next village for lunch and then walk back again – hopefully with one or two detours on the way back.

'That would have been nice, *chicita*,' Miguel smiled regretfully when Stella mentioned her plans. 'But I am already busy today. A previous arrangement, I'm afraid.'

'But it's really important,' said Stella. Talk about unfair! She felt she was at a disadvantage anyway, and now this!

'Sorry,' shrugged Miguel. 'It'll have to wait. But I'll see you tonight, won't I? Down in the village?'

Stella watched Miguel go out the door. OK, so she didn't get to spend her allotted time with him but it wasn't the end of the world and certainly not the end of things between Mig and herself. He said he'd see her tonight, hadn't he? Which suggested he didn't have plans to spend exclusive time with either Jodie and Ushi. Yeah, to hell with today. It was this evening that was all-important! Stella smiled to herself. She'd make herself look so sexy and gorgeous, he simply wouldn't be able to resist her.

With Miguel out of the way, the girls spent the day preparing themselves for their big night out and indulged themselves in a mammoth make-over-and-make-up fest. They decided to ban any chat about Miguel but it was inevitable that little snippets would slip through.

'I don't think I'll wear that much slap,' considered Jodie, after some deliberation. 'I think Miguel will prefer a more natural look.'

'Oh do you?' said Ushi, applying another layer of lippy. 'Well that's not the impression I get. I reckon he wants a glam girl who'll really stand out from the crowd.'

'And you reckon you're her, do you?' muttered Jodie. 'Well you're wrong. So very wrong. You see . . .'

Jodie broke off suddenly as Stella walked proudly into the room. Dressed in a tight crimson number with her dark hair pinned up high, she looked stunning. There was no other word for it.

'Aunt Maria lent it to me,' Stella trilled, whirling herself around and around. 'It used to belong to her. What do you think?'

Normally, Jodie and Ushi would have been wowing all over her, telling her the truth – that she looked truly a-mazing. But this wasn't 'normally'. This was tantamount to war! And seeing Stella standing there in such a fabulous dress caused the competitive juices to start flowing even more.

'Uhmmm, not bad,' muttered Jodie and furiously started applying lipstick while Ushi didn't say anything but suddenly deciding that her favourite jeans weren't quite the thing after all, promptly changed into a mini skirt.

'Well I think I look fab,' said Stella huffily. 'And d'know what? I'm pretty damed sure that Miguel will, too. When he sees me in this, he just won't be able to keep his eyes – or his hands – off me. I'd throw the towel in if I were you, girls. You'll see . . .'

She preened herself in the mirror. 'Quality will out!'

'Yeah?' muttered Ushi, elbowing her out of the way. 'Well if that's the case, you may as well forget all about it, right now!'

Before a shocked Stella could think of a sufficiently cutting reply, Jodie had her say.

'I'd both forget it, if I were you,' she said. 'There's only one winner around here. And you're both looking at her!'

Ushi tapped her foot impatiently and looked around the village square. They'd been here for ages and still no Miguel. Just where had he got to? She glanced at Jodie whose eyes seemed permanently fixed on the door. Momentarily they flickered towards Ushi. Ushi looked away. They'd barely spoken since leaving the house while Stella seemed to have well and truly disappeared into the bosom of her family! She'd hardly left Aunt Maria's side.

Suddenly Ushi heard Jodie sigh with obvious relief. Ushi looked around the room. About time! Miguel had finally arrived and was talking to his mum and Stella by the buffet table on the other side of the room. Thinking that she just might be a bit hungry, Ushi sidled over there – followed at a discreet distance by Jodie.

Purposefully hovering next to the plates of *tortilla* while sneaking little glances at the Rodriguez family group, suddenly she saw Aunt Maria's hands fly up to her face while Stella's usually olivey complexion took on a definite chalky hue. Ushi was intrigued. Just what the hell was going on? The next thing she knew, a slight dark girl had joined their group. Ushi felt rooted to the spot as she watched Miguel put his arm around her, undeniably protectively. She heard Jodie give a slight yell and only just managed to stifle one herself. Then, unbelievably, Miguel was beckoning them both over.

'Hi Ushi, Jodie . . .' he said, with a smile. 'There's someone I'd like you to meet. This is Juanita, my fiancée. We've just got engaged!'

If the train from Barcelona to Valle d'Aran had seemed to have taken forever, then the train from Valle d'Aran to Lloret seemed to take an eternity – and then some! Of course it didn't help that Ushi, Jodie and Stella just happened to be travelling in silence.

After Miguel's announcement, they'd called a truce. But it had proved to only be temporary. Once back at Aunt Maria's, they'd discussed 'the Miguel madness' in more detail and it had all come out. How Jodie had just happened to mention Davy and Tomas to Miguel and how Ushi had let slip about Max.

Stella, who felt herself to be the innocent party in all this, had declared herself shocked and very hurt.

'How could you both?' she'd asked. 'After all we said at the beginning . . . The rules we made.'

'Sorry,' Ushi had muttered. 'I guess it was a really dumb thing to do.'

Jodie had also apologised but Stella hadn't been moved. They had, however, agreed on one thing. It was time to leave Valle d'Aran.

Staring out of the window as the train chugged its way down a steep hillside, Jodie felt she had to say something. She had to clear the air. They had little more than a week left but the bad atmosphere that had grown up between them was threatening to ruin it all.

'Look,' she began, turning towards Stella. 'Can't we forget all about it? Put it behind us? It was a mistake. Ushi and I have apologised. What else can we do?'

Stella eventually returned her gaze. 'I dunno . . . I know I should forgive you but it's hard. I feel kind of betrayed.'

'You're right,' Ushi suddenly piped up. 'But we all betrayed ourselves, really, didn't we? All that guff we spoke about it not spoiling our friendship – whatever the outcome. And what was the outcome, for God's sake? *None* of us ended up with him, yet we're still scrapping about it. I can't believe we've let a lad come between us like this.'

'It got completely out of hand,' agreed Jodie. 'And so competitive. Now you were guilty of that, too, Stell. You have to admit that.'

Stella looked at them both. 'Oh alright,' she said. 'It's just that . . . Oh, I don't know. I feel such a fool. I mean what d'you think Miguel thinks of us now?'

'Who cares?' shrugged Ushi. 'It doesn't really matter, though does it? None of us did anything with him we need to regret. Just said a few daft things, that's all. To be honest, he seemed pretty bemused by the whole situation. Maybe he thought it was a giant wind-up.'

'I, er, snogged him,' said Jodie in a quiet little voice.

'What???!!!!' exclaimed Ushi. 'You never told us that!'

Jodie grinned. 'I wasn't allowed to, was I? One of our daft rules, remember?'

'What was it like?' Stella couldn't stop herself asking.

Jodie started to laugh. 'Not that great, actually. Max was tons more talented. And I bet Tomas was too! You know, Stell, you cousin's looks promised a lot more than they were actually able to deliver.'

Stella nodded. 'You know something else? Thinking about it, I don't think he was that great after all. It's probably just 'cos we were bored and didn't fancy the prospect of a few flirt free days.'

'Yeah,' added Ushi. 'Well, it's about time all that changed. I've had enough of lads! From now on, I say we do exactly what *we* want to do. The male sex can take a running jump!'

'What, even old Snake Hips?' asked Stella. 'What would happen if your insurance policy suddenly matured and darlin' Davy appeared?'

Ushi shuddered. 'Don't even think about it! I don't want to know. Us girlies – that's the only thing I'm interested in now – and sod the post-holiday blues. We come first with each other, right?'

Stella and Jodie grinned. 'Absolutely!'

They found a happening little campsite on the outskirts of Lloret which was directly on the beach. Eager to hit the sand and surf, they decided to put the tent up later rather than straight away. They were just strolling through the Bar-B-Q and recreation area when Ushi stopped dead in her tracks.

'What's wrong, Ush?' asked Stella. 'You look like you've just seen a ghost.'

Ushi couldn't speak but managed to point to the tennis courts.

'Ohmigod!' muttered Jodie. 'Talk about Smarm Features and tempting fate!'

Absorbed in a game of doubles were the ferry-nerds and another equally geeky-looking bloke.

'Look, look over there,' Ushi eventually managed to squeak.

'Ohmigod,' muttered Stella. 'Let's get the hell out of here. And quick!'

Rushing back to their pitch, they were laughing so much they could hardly stand. They picked up their tent and legged it out of the site.

'So what now?' Jodie said once they were back on the road. 'Do we wait for a bus?'

'No fear!' replied Ushi. 'No, we get a cab back into town. And hey, we'll book into a hotel. Let's live a little!'

Stella stood in the road and hailed a passing taxi.

'Let's get the hell out of here – like, NOW!'

✶Dear Ushi, Jodie and Stella✶
Sending ourselves a postcard?
Great idea - eh? But it's just
a little something to cheer us
all up when the post-holiday
blues have kicked in with a
vengeance. What larks! What
laughs! And what lads! It
wasn't all plain sailing, but
what the hell? We had fun,
we learnt a lot, and most
important of all - after
everything we've been through-
we're still mates. The best of.
So here's to next year!
Lots of love ♡xxx♡
    Stella, Jodie and Ushi
      xx   xx   xx

J·17

Subscription offer

12 issues for the price of 11!

Get your fave mag delivered to your door every blimmin' month for a year and never miss a copy! How? Simply complete your details and return this coupon with your payment to *J17* Subcriptions Department, Tower House, Sovereign Park, Market Harborough, Leicestershire LE16 9EF.

☐ **I enclose a cheque/postal order made payable to *J17* magazine for £16.50**

Please debit my Access/Visa/Amex/Diners

☐☐☐☐☐☐☐☐☐☐☐☐☐☐☐☐

Expiry date _____ Signature _____

Date _____

Name _____

Address _____

_____ Postcode _____

Or phone the Subscriptions Orders Hotline

01858 435339

Between 9.30am and 5.30pm Monday to Friday

Offer closes 30 June 1998 and is open to UK residents only

WA19